Amelia Edith Huddleston Bar

The Young People of Shakespeare's Dramas

Amelia Edith Huddleston Bar

The Young People of Shakespeare's Dramas

ISBN/EAN: 9783337394172

Printed in Europe, USA, Canada, Australia, Japan

Cover: Foto ©Andreas Hilbeck / pixelio.de

More available books at **www.hansebooks.com**

THE YOUNG PEOPLE

OF

SHAKESPEARE'S DRAMAS.

FOR YOUTHFUL READERS.

BY

AMELIA E. BARR.

" He who takes us from the smoke and stir of every-day toil, and laps us in the Elysium of our boyish days—blood-stirring and hopeful—is a benefactor to his species ; and to no mortal do we more owe this reminiscence and gratitude than to WILLIAM SHAKESPEARE."

NEW YORK:

D. APPLETON AND COMPANY.

1, 3, AND 5 BOND STREET.

1882.

PREFACE.

AMONG the things which make this age re-
markable is the excellence of its literature for
young people. The brightest intellects, the
most delicate fancies, the cleverest pencils, are
engaged in this service. Everything that is
lovely and of good report receives individuality,
and is set to allure into the paths of virtue and
nobleness. No more perfect and gracious types
of youthful life exist than the few scattered
(mainly) through Shakespeare's Historical Dramas ; and surely they may most fitly introduce
young readers into that splendid world of the
imagination which the great poet created for us.

In bringing them to the front of each drama,
some characters not necessary to the youthful

history or the action of the story have been
omitted ; but the text has always been used with
that reverent care which must result from forty
years of loving study of the Shakespearean plays.

L. I.

CONTENTS.

ILLUSTRATIONS.

*The Illustrations are by Sir John Gilbert, from the
Staunton Shakespeare.*

ARTHUR PLANTAGENET,

DUKE OF BRITTANY.

PERSONS IN THE DRAMA.

JOHN.—*King of England.*
PHILIP.—*King of France.*
ARTHUR.—*Duke of Brittany.*
LEWIS.—*Dauphin of France.*
PANDULPH.—*The Pope's Legate.*
HUBERT DE BURGH.—*Chamberlain to John.*
SALISBURY. ⎫
PEMBROKE. ⎬ *English Lords.*
BIGOT. ⎭
FAULCONBRIDGE.—*A Friend of King John's.*
CONSTANCE.—*Duchess of Brittany.   Mother of Arthur.*
ELINOR.—*Mother of King John.*
BLANCH.—*John's Niece.*
      Attendants on Hubert de Burgh.

ARTHUR PLANTAGENET,

IT must surely be a very pleasant thought to young people that Shakespeare did not leave the splendid world of his imagination without children. It is true that, except in the play of "King John," no very important part is assigned them; but they have all a positive individuality, and the English historical dramas contain some lovely types of boyhood—clear, single characters, full of a childish sincerity.

Indeed, Shakespeare has given us no lovelier picture than that of the fair and unfortunate Prince Arthur, upon whose fate the whole interest of the drama of "King John" turns; and an added pathos clings to the character, because it was drawn shortly after the death of Shakespeare's only son, Hammet, and may have been in some measure a transcription of the lost child's beauty and amiability, and of his father's grief.

The Arthur of " King John" was the son of Geffrey, the brother of Richard I, King of England. He inherited the throne of England both through the right of his father and the will of his uncle; but, upon the death of Richard, John seized the throne. Then Constance, the mother of Arthur, procured the protection of Philip Augustus, King of France, who pledged himself to maintain the cause of the wronged prince, and the play opens with the demand of Chatillon, the French Ambassador, for Arthur's rights:

CHAT. Philip of France, in right and true behalf
Of thy deceased brother Geffrey's son,
Arthur Plantagenet, lays most lawful claim
To this fair island, and the territories;
To Ireland, Poictiers, Anjou, Touraine, Maine:
Desiring thee to lay aside the sword,
Which sways usurpingly these several titles,
And put the same into young Arthur's hand,
Thy nephew and right royal sovereign.

K. JOHN. What follows if we disallow of this?

CHAT. The proud control of fierce and bloody war,
To enforce these rights so forcibly withheld.

K. JOHN. Here have we war for war, and blood
    for blood,
Controlment for controlment: so answer France.
  CHAT. Then take my king's defiance from my
    mouth,
The furthest limit of my embassy.
  K. JOHN. Bear mine to him, and so depart in peace :
Be thou as lightning in the eyes of France ;
For ere thou canst report I will be there,
The thunder of my cannon shall be heard ;
So, hence ! Be thou the trumpet of our wrath,
And sullen presage of your own decay.
An honorable conduct let him have :—
Pembroke, look to it. Farewell, Chatillon.

During this scene Elinor, the mother of
King John and the grandmother of Arthur,
was present. She was an arrogant, bad woman,
who hated her daughter-in-law Constance, and
who scorned to make apologies, even to her
own conscience, for her cruelty and injustice.
John tried to justify his position.

Our strong possession, and our right, for us,

he exclaimed ; but Elinor answered, proudly :

Your strong possession much more than your right;
Or else it must go wrong with you and me.

The second act takes us into the very heat of the conflict. The two armies met under the walls of Angiers. With the French were Constance and Arthur, Philip and the Dauphin, and their ally the Archduke of Austria. With the English were King John, his mother Elinor, and his niece Blanch of Castile. Before the walls of Angiers there was a stormy interview, during which Elinor and Constance came to words as sharp as blows. Their quarrel was interrupted by the Dauphin, who impatiently said:

Women and fools, break off your conference.
King John, this is the very sum of all—
England and Ireland, Anjou, Touraine, Maine,
In right of Arthur do I claim of thee:
Wilt thou resign them, and lay down thine arms?
 K. JOHN. My life as soon:—I do defy thee,
   France.
Arthur of Bretagne, yield thee to my hand;
And, out of my dear love, I'll give thee more
Than e'er the coward hand of France can win:
Submit thee, boy.
 ELI. Come to thy grandam, child.
 CONST. Do, child, go to it' grandam, child:
Give grandam kingdom, and it' grandam will

Give it a plum, a cherry, and a fig:
There's a good grandam.

In this violent scene we get the first glimpse
of the lovely and loving nature of the boy
prince. He is pained and shocked at the quarrel between his grandmother and mother, and,
weeping, cries:

ARTHUR.   Good my mother, peace!
I would that I were low laid in my grave:
I am not worth this coil that's made for me.

The next movement in Arthur's fate ex-
hibits the poor boy as a mere puppet in the
hands of the two kings, to be used for their
mutual advantage. For they soon perceive
that nothing is to be gained by fighting, so
they become reconciled, and, to cement their
alliance, arrange a marriage between Philip's
son, the Dauphin Lewis, and John's niece,
Blanch of Castile. But it is not until the arrangements have been completed that King
Philip remembers Constance and Arthur, and
asks:

K. PHI. Is not the Lady Constance in this troop?
I know she is not; for this match, made up,

Her presence would have interrupted much :
Where is she and her son? tell me, who knows.

> LEWIS. She is sad and passionate at your highness'
> tent.

> K. PHI. And, by my faith, this league, that we
> have made,

Will give her sadness very little cure.
Brother of England, how may we content
This widow lady? In her right we came;
Which we, God knows, have turned another way,
To our own vantage.

> K. JOHN. We will heal up all,

For we'll create young Arthur duke of Bretagne,
And earl of Richmond; and this fair town
We'll make him lord of. Call the lady Constance;
Some speedy messenger bid her repair
To our solemnity.

William Longsword, Earl of Salisbury, is
sent to give Constance this unwelcome invitation.
At first she will not credit the treason of the
King of France. "It is not so," she answers.
"Gone to be married! Gone to swear a peace!
Gone to be friends! It is not so." She has a
king's oath to the contrary; she is sure that
Salisbury has misspoke or misheard; and with
a terrified petulance she threatens Salisbury—

Thou shalt be punish'd for thus frighting me,
For I am sick and capable of fears;
Oppress'd with wrongs, and therefore full of fears;
A widow, husbandless, subject to fears;
A woman, naturally born to fears;
And though thou now confess thou didst but jest,
With my vex'd spirits I can not take a truce,
But they will quake and tremble all this day.

Salisbury is full of sympathy for the injured prince and his mother, but it is the child only that recognizes it. When Constance bids him "begone," and says, "she can not brook his sight," the gentle-hearted Arthur is grieved and saddened by all this discord of quarrel, and says:

I do beseech you, madam, be content.

The next scene shows us the two kings in the presence of Constance, whom they vainly endeavor to reconcile to the alliance they have made. The argument is interrupted by the entrance of Pandulph, the Pope's Legate, who brings an order to King John for the reinstatement of Stephen Langton as Archbishop of Canterbury. This order John absolutely refuses to obey. He answers:

> No Italian priest
> Shall tithe or toll in our dominions;

and Pandulph immediately curses and excommunicates him.   This sentence at once breaks the new-made peace, for Pandulph orders Philip:

> On peril of a curse,
> Let go the hand of that arch-heretic;
> And raise the power of France upon his head
> Unless he do submit himself to Rome.

In the engagement which ensues the French are defeated, and Arthur is taken prisoner by John.   We see the child next surrounded by his grandmother Elinor, his uncle John, Hubert de Burgh—John's chamberlain—and other English lords.   The boy in his innocent helplessness stands like a lamb among wolves.   His cruel, crafty uncle, indeed, bids him "not to look sad," and promises—

> Thy grandam loves thee, and thy uncle will
> As dear be to thee as thy father was;

but in this dreadful hour Arthur is not thinking of himself; his one ejaculation of sorrow is for his mother:

> O, this will make my mother die with grief.

Then, with this promise to be "a father" to the boy on his lips, John turns to Hubert de Burgh, and, with subtile flatteries and promises, prompts him to do the deed he is ashamed to name. He is afraid to say too much, he is afraid he does not say enough, but at last he mutters:

K. JOHN. Good Hubert, Hubert, Hubert, throw
     thine eye
On yond' young boy: I'll tell thee what, my friend,
He is a very serpent in my way;
And wheresoe'er this foot of mine doth tread
He lies before me:—Dost thou understand me?
Thou art his keeper.

HUB.   And I'll keep him so,
That he shall not offend your majesty.

K. JOHN. Death.

HUB.   My Lord?

K. JOHN.   A Grave.

HUB.   He shall not live.

K. JOHN.   Enough.
I could be merry now: Hubert, I love thee;
Well, I'll not say what I intend for thee:
Remember.

Alas! poor Constance knows that her little son has gone to death. Is he not in the power

of men "fit for bloody villainy"? She enters
the presence of King Philip, Lewis, and Pandulph in such distraction of grief as makes
them fear she "utters madness and not sorrow."
"Grief," she cries:

Grief fills the room up of my absent child,
Lies in his bed, walks up and down with me,
Puts on his pretty looks, repeats his words,
Remembers me of all his gracious parts.

.   .   .   .   .   .

My boy, my Arthur, my fair son!
My life, my joy, my food, my all the world!
My widow-comfort, and my sorrow's cure!

Not once dares she to hope that she will see
him again on earth; neither Philip nor Lewis
can offer her any comfort; she turns to Pandulph for the only consolation left her; and
in a tearful passion of tenderness cries:

Father Cardinal, I have heard you say
That we shall see and know our friends in heaven:
If that be true, I shall see my boy again;
For, since the birth of Cain, the first male child,
To him that did but yesterday suspire,
There was not such a gracious creature born.

In the next act we are told that the " Lady
Constance in a frenzy died"; and history places
her death so soon after Arthur's captivity that
we may well suppose it was hastened by grief
for the loss of this gracious child.

We next see Arthur a prisoner in Northampton Castle. Hubert de Burgh has received
orders to burn out his eyes, and, struggling
between an habitual service and a half-awak-
ened love and pity for his captive, he prepares to obey them. The scene that follows
is one of incomparable beauty and pathos, and
would be almost too tragic if we did not feel
from the very first that Hubert will not touch
the boy's sight, "for all the treasure that his
uncle owes."

SCENE.—Northampton. *A Room in the Castle.*

Enter HUBERT *and Two* Attendants.

HUB. Heat me these irons hot; and look thou stand
Within the arras; when I strike my foot
Upon the bosom of the ground, rush forth,
And bind the boy, which you will find with me,
Fast to the chair: be heedful: hence, and watch.

  1 ATTEND. I hope your warrant will bear out the
    deed.

HUB. Uncleanly scruples!   Fear not you: look
   to 't.   [*Exeunt* Attendants.
Young lad, come forth; I have to say with you.
                 ·   *Enter* ARTHUR.

ARTHUR. Good morrow, Hubert.

HUB.   Good morrow, little prince.

ARTH. As little prince (having so great a title
To be more prince) as may be.—You are sad.

HUB. Indeed, I have been merrier.

ARTH.   Mercy on me!
Methinks nobody should be sad but I:
Yet I remember, when I was in France,
Young gentlemen would be as sad as night,
Only for wantonness.   By my christendom,*
So I were out of prison, and kept sheep,
I should be merry as the day is long;
And so I would be here, but that I doubt
My uncle practices more harm to me:
He is afraid of me, and I of him:
Is it my fault that I was Geffrey's son?
No, indeed, is't not; And I would to heaven
I were your son, so you would love me, Hu-
   bert.

HUB. [*Aside.*] If I talk to him with his innocent
   prate

---

* Here Arthur prettily asseverates by his baptismal rite, or his
Christening.

He will awake my mercy, which lies dead:
Therefore I will be sudden, and dispatch.

ARTH. Are you sick, Hubert? you look pale to-
day:
In sooth I would you were a little sick;
That I might sit all night, and watch with you:
I warrant, I love you more than you do me.

HUB. [*Aside.*] His words do take possession of
my bosom.—
Read here, young Arthur. (*Showing a paper.*)
[*Aside.*] How now, foolish rheum!
Turning dispiteous torture out of doors!
I must be brief, lest resolution drop
Out at mine eyes, in tender womanish tears.
Can you not read it? is it not fair writ?

ARTH. Too fairly, Hubert, for so foul effect;
Must you with hot irons burn out both mine eyes?

HUB. Young boy, I must.

ARTH.   And will you?

HUB.   And I will.

ARTH. Have you the heart? When your head
did but ache,
I knit my handkerchief about your brows
(The best I had, a princess wrought it me),
And I did never ask it you again:
And with my hand at midnight held your head;
And, like the watchful minutes to the hour,

Still and anon cheer'd up the heavy time:
Saying, "What lack you?" and, "Where lies your
    grief?"
Or, "What good love may I perform for you?"
Many a poor man's son would have lain still,
And ne'er have spoke a loving word to you;
But you at your sick service had a prince.
Nay, you may think my love was crafty love,
And call it cunning; do, an if you will;
If heaven be pleased that you must use me ill,
Why, then you must.—Will you put out mine eyes?
These eyes, that never did, nor never shall,
So much as frown on you?

HUB.   I have sworn to do it;
And with hot irons must I burn them out.

ARTH. Ah, none, but in this iron age, would do it;
The iron of itself, though heat red-hot,
Approaching near these eyes, would drink my tears,
And quench his fiery indignation
Even in the matter of mine innocence:
Nay, after that, consume away in rust,
But for containing fire to harm mine eye.
Are you more stubborn-hard than hammer'd iron;
An if an angel should have come to me,
And told me, Hubert should put out mine eyes,
I would not have believ'd him; no tongue, but
    Hubert's.

HUB. Come forth.　　　　　　　　　　[*Stamps.*

Re-enter Attendants, *with Cords, Irons, etc.*

Do as I bid you do.

ARTH. O, save me, Hubert, save me; my eyes are
　　out,

Even with the fierce looks of these bloody men.

HUB. Give me the iron, I say, and bind him here.

ARTH. Alas! what need you be so boisterous
　　rough?

I will not struggle, I will stand stone still.

For heaven's sake, Hubert, let me not be bound!

Nay, hear me, Hubert! drive these men away,

And I will sit as quiet as a lamb;

I will not stir, nor wince, nor speak a word,

Nor look upon the iron angerly:

Thrust but these men away, and I'll forgive you,

Whatever torment you do put me to.

HUB. Go, stand within; let me alone with him,

1 ATTEND. I am best pleas'd to be from such a
　　deed.　　　　　　　　[*Exeunt* Attendants.

ARTH. Alas! I then have chid away my friend;

He hath a stern look, but a gentle heart;—

Let him come back, that his compassion may

Give life to yours.

HUB.　　　　　　Come, boy, prepare yourself.

ARTH. Is there no remedy?

HUB.　　　　　　None, but to lose your eyes.

ARTH. O heaven!—that there were but a mote
　　in yours,
A grain, a dust, a gnat, a wandering hair,
Any annoyance in that precious sense!
Then, feeling what small things are boist'rous there,
Your vile intent must needs seem horrible.

HUB. Is this your promise? go to, hold your
　　tongue.

ARTH. Hubert, the utterance of a brace of tongues
Must needs want pleading for a pair of eyes;
Let me not hold my tongue; let me not, Hubert!
Or, Hubert, if you will, cut out my tongue,
So I may keep mine eyes: O spare mine eyes;
Though to no use, but still to look on you!
Lo, by my troth, the instrument is cold,
And would not harm me.

HUB.　　　　　　　　　　I can heat it, boy.

ARTH. No, in good sooth; the fire is dead with
　　grief,
Being create for comfort, to be us'd
In undeserved extremes: See else yourself;
There is no malice in this burning coal;
The breath of heaven hath blown his spirit out,
And strew'd repentant ashes on his head.

HUB. But with my breath I can revive it, boy.

ARTH. And if you do, you will but make it blush,
And glow with shame of your proceedings, Hubert;

Nay, it, perchance, will sparkle in your eyes;
And, like a dog that is compell'd to fight,
Snatch at his master that doth tarre him on.
All things, that you should use to do me wrong,
Deny their office; only you do lack
That mercy which fierce fire and iron extends,
Creatures of note for mercy-lacking uses.

HUB. Well, see to live; I will not touch thine eyes
For all the treasure that thine uncle owes:
Yet am I sworn, and I did purpose, boy,
With this same very iron to burn them out.

ARTH. O, now you look like Hubert! all this while
You were disguised.

HUB.   Peace: no more. Adieu:
Your uncle must not know but you are dead:
I'll fill these dogged spies with false reports.
And, pretty child, sleep doubtless, and secure,
That Hubert, for the wealth of all the world,
Will not offend thee.

ARTH. O heaven!—I thank you, Hubert.

HUB. Silence; no more: Go closely in with me;
Much danger do I undergo for thee.   [*Exeunt.*

In the next scene we are made aware of the
general discontent of the "distempered lords,"
and barons of England, with John's government; and it finds vent in a demand for Ar-

2

thur's release from prison. The earls of Salisbury and Pembroke are the spokesmen on this
occasion, and they "heartily request"

Th' enfranchisement of Arthur; whose restraint
Doth move the murmuring lips of discontent
To break into this dangerous argument.—
If, what in rest you have, in right you hold,
Why then your fears (which, as they say, attend
The steps of wrong), should move you to mew up
Your tender kinsman, and to choke his days
With barbarous ignorance, and deny his youth
The rich advantage of good exercise?
That the time's enemies may not have this
To grace occasions, let it be our suit,
That you have bid us ask his liberty;
Which for our goods we do no further ask,
Than whereupon our weal, on you depending,
Counts it your weal, he have his liberty.

Even while Pembroke is speaking, Hubert
enters, and privately tells John that Arthur is
dead; and the earls, noting Hubert's face and
John's changing color, suspect the news even
before the king says:

K. JOHN. We can not hold mortality's strong
     hand:—

Good lords, although my will to give is living,
The suit which you demand is gone and dead:
He tells us, Arthur is deceas'd to-night.

· " Indeed," answers Salisbury, with that bitter sarcasm which is the first expression of
subdued rage:

SALIS. Indeed, we fear'd his sickness was past cure.
PEM. Indeed, we heard how near his death he was
Before the child himself felt he was sick:
This must be answered, either here, or hence.

K. JOHN. Why do you bend such solemn brows
on me?
Think you I bear the shears of destiny?
Have I commandment on the pulse of life?

SALIS. It is apparent foul play; and 'tis shame,
That greatness should so grossly offer it:
So thrive it in your game! and so, farewell.

PEM. Stay yet, Lord Salisbury; I'll go with thee,
And find the inheritance of this poor child,
His little kingdom of a forced grave.
That blood which ow'd the breadth of all this isle,
Three foot of it doth hold; Bad world the while!
This must not be thus borne.

The departure of the angry lords is followed
by a messenger bringing news of the death of

John's mother, and of the landing of a large
French army in England under the Dauphin.
To these bad tidings are added the unfavorable
predictions of a prophet in Pomfret, and the
supernatural appearance of five moons in the
sky; and Hubert tells John that,

> Old men, and beldams, in the streets,
> Do prophecy upon it dangerously:
> Young Arthur's death is common in their mouths:
> And when they talk of him, they shake their
> heads,
> And whisper one another in the ear.

Then John, like a craven, turns upon Hubert, and seeks to throw upon him the whole
blame of Arthur's death—of that "deed which
both tongues held too vile to name." He
orders Hubert out of his sight, whimpering:

> My nobles leave me; and my state is brav'd,
> Even at my gates, with ranks of foreign powers.

And when Hubert confesses "Young Arthur
is alive," John's feelings are purely selfish.
He cares not that he has escaped the sin of
murdering an innocent child, but he rejoices
because the news may bring back to his stand-

ard the revolted and angry lords. " Doth
Arthur live?" he cries.

> O, haste thee to the peers,
> Throw this report on their incensed rage,
>
> .   .   .   .   .   .
>
> O, answer not; but to my closet bring
> The angry lords, with all expedient haste;
> I conjure thee but slowly; run more fast.

Unfortunately, while Hubert is with the
king, Arthur, distracted with fears, resolves to
make an effort to escape by leaping from the
walls of the castle.

> ARTH. The wall is high, and yet will I leap
>   down :—
> Good ground, be pitiful, and hurt me not!—
> There's few, or none, do know me; if they did,
> This ship boy's semblance hath disguis'd me quite.
> I am afraid; and yet I'll venture it.
> If I get down, and do not break my limbs,
> I'll find a thousand shifts to get away:
> As good to die, and go, as die and stay.
>   [*Leaps down.*
> O me! my uncle's spirit is in these stones—
> Heaven take my soul, and England keep my bones!

While the poor little mangled body is still beneath the walls, Salisbury and Pembroke find it; and Pembroke cries out:

O death, made proud with pure and princely beauty!
The earth had not a hole to hide this deed;

while Salisbury kneels before that "ruin of sweet life," and vows:

Never to taste the pleasures of the world,
Never to be infected with delight,
Nor conversant with ease and idleness,
'Till I have set a glory to this hand,
By giving it the worship of revenge.

At this moment Hubert, bearing the king's message, that "Arthur still lives," approaches and finds them lamenting over the prince's corpse. Bigot, Earl of Norfolk, asks him, passionately, "Who kill'd this prince?" and Hubert answers:

'Tis not an hour since I left him well:
I honor'd him, I lov'd him; and will weep
My date of life out, for his sweet life's loss.

Even John's stanch and unfaltering friend, Philip Faulconbridge, abhors the deed, and tells Hubert:

There is not yet so ugly a fiend of hell
As thou shalt be, if thou didst kill this child.
    HUB. Upon my soul,—
    FAUL.   If thou didst but consent
To this most cruel act, do but despair,
And, if thou want'st a cord, the smallest thread
That ever spider twisted from her womb
Will serve to strangle thee; a rush will be
A beam to hang thee on; or would'st thou drown
        thyself,
Put but a little water in a spoon,
And it shall be as all the ocean,
Enough to stifle such a villain up.—
I do suspect thee very grievously.
    HUB. If I in act, consent, or sin of thought
Be guilty of the stealing that sweet breath
Which was embounded in this beauteous clay,
Let hell want pains enough to torture me!
I left him well.
    FAUL.   Go, bear him in thy arms.—
How easy dost thou take all England up!
From forth this morsel of dead royalty,
The life, the right, and truth of all this realm
Is fled to heaven.

After Arthur's death John stumbles forward
through humiliations, treason, and defeat, to

his own wretched end; and dies at last, the victim of some monkish revenge, with a horrible poison in his veins.

King David, many centuries before John lived, declared that "bloody and deceitful men should not live out half their days," and Shakespeare puts into John's lips the same verdict on a crafty, cruel life; for when he was scorned by his revolted lords, and terrified by foreign invasion and supernatural prodigies, he whispered to himself:

> There is no sure foundation set on blood;
> No certain life achiev'd by others' death.

HISTORICAL SKETCH

OF

PRINCE ARTHUR OF BRITTANY.

ARTHUR OF BRITTANY was but the heir to
a tragedy which had shadowed his mother's
whole life, and which claimed him also from
his very birth. For Constance, being Duchess
of Brittany in her own right, had been even
in her infancy the object of England's envy
and rapacity. At three years of age Henry
the Second took her by force, and contracted
her in marriage to his son Geffrey, thus in-
suring, as he thought, the duchy of Brittany
to his own posterity. For sixteen years she
was kept in a species of constraint—more a
hostage than a sovereign—but in her nineteenth
year the marriage was formally celebrated, and
she was recognized as Duchess of Brittany by
two acts of legislation, still preserved, and
bearing her own seal and signature.

Geffrey, however, did not live long; he was killed at a tournament, and Arthur was born shortly after his death, A. D. 1188. The child's birth filled Brittany with joy. The people insisted that he should be named Arthur, after the famous hero of that country, who, though dead for six centuries, was still confidently expected to return; and, in the wonderful personal beauty of this son of Constance, they saw with a fond credulity the earnest of their hopes.

But Henry of England immediately demanded the custody of the child; and, upon Constance's spirited refusal, he invaded Brittany, devastated the whole country with fire and sword, and forcibly married Constance to the Earl of Carlisle, conferring on him the duchy of Brittany, to be held as a fief of the English crown. However, as soon as Henry died, the barons of Brittany rose in revolt, and drove Chester and his English followers out of the country.

Then Richard Cœur-de-Lion ascended the English throne. One of his first deeds was to contract the little prince Arthur, then only two years old, in marriage with the daughter of

Tancred, King of Sicily. Richard received on
this occasion a dowry of twenty thousand gold-
en *oncie*, which the Sicilian king paid in ad-
vance; and he at this time formally recognized Arthur as "our most dear nephew, and
heir, if by chance we should die without
issue."

Therefore, when Richard did die without
issue, in A. D. 1199, Arthur was the legitimate
heir of all his dominions. But John produced
a testament by which Richard gave him the
crown of England. Then Constance placed
herself and Arthur under the guardianship of
Philip Augustus, King of France. Arthur being
then eleven years of age, Philip solemnly engaged to maintain his rights against John, and
it is at this crisis in Arthur's fate that the
play of "King John" opens.

Arthur, however, was but a puppet in the
hands of the crafty Philip, to be set up or
knocked down, as Philip desired to bully or
cajole John out of the territories of the house
of Anjou. In Arthur's person he had a hostage whom he could put forward as an ally,
or degrade as a prisoner; and in the same
spirit, when he seized a fortress in the name of

Arthur, he demolished it, that he might lose no opportunity of destroying a barrier to the extension of his own frontier. The peace which Shakespeare represents as being established by the marriage of Blanch and Lewis is historically true; it took place May 22, A. D. 1200.

After the peace of A. D. 1200 Arthur remained under the care of King Philip, in fear, it is said, of the treachery of his uncle John. Constance's grief may not have been overdrawn, for she died the next year, and, therefore, did not witness the wretched end of her beloved son. And the peace between France and England was broken within two years; and once again the unhappy Arthur was made to raise the banner of war against his powerful uncle. With a small force he marched against the town of Mirebeau, where his grandmother Elinor was stationed; and John, who was in Normandy, being apprised of the danger of his mother, "used such diligence that he was upon his enemies' necks ere they could understand anything of his coming." The town was taken by treachery, Arthur captured and sent a prisoner to the Castle of Falaise.

It was in this dark prison house that the

attempt was made to deprive Arthur of his
sight. But says Holinshed in his Chronicle,
"through such resistance as he made against
one of the tormentors that came to execute
the king's command, and such lamentable words
as he uttered, Hubert de Burgh did preserve
him from that injury, not doubting but rather
to have thanks than displeasure at the king's
hands for delivering him of such infamy as
would have redounded unto his highness if the
young prince had been so cruelly dealt with.
Certain it is that in the year next ensuing he was
removed from Falaise into the Castle of Rouen,
out of which there was not any that would
confess that ever he saw him go alive. Some
have written that as he essayed to have escaped out of prison, and proving to climb over
the walls of the castle, he fell into the river
Seine and was drowned."

All things considered, it is most likely that
Arthur perished at Rouen. The darkest of the
stories connected with his death is that which
makes him, on the night of the 3d of April,
1203, awakened from his sleep, and led to the
foot of the Castle of Rouen, which the Seine
washed. There, say the French historians, he

entered a boat, in which sate John, and Peter de Maulac, his esquire. Terror took possession of the unhappy boy, and he threw himself at his uncle's feet; but John with his own hand slew his nephew, and the deep waters of the river received his corpse.

The quarrel between the Pope and John did not really take place until A. D. 1207, four years after Arthur's death; and the invasion of England by the Dauphin until A. D. 1216; but Shakespeare has leaped over the barriers of time, and made the death of John, with its attending circumstances of domestic revolt and foreign invasion, rapidly follow the death of Arthur. This was necessary in an historical drama, where it would be as unreasonable to expect absolute historical accuracy as it would be to require an artist to give us the exact relative positions of every bay and promontory. We must remember the historical plays of Shakespeare stand in the same relation to the historic events they deal with that a landscape painting does to a map.

EDWARD PLANTAGENET,

SON OF KING HENRY VI.

PERSONS IN THE DRAMA.

HENRY VI.—*King of England.*
EDWARD.—*Son of Henry VI.*
DUKE OF YORK.—*Protector.*
EDWARD.—*Afterward* EDWARD IV.
CLARENCE.
RICHARD. } *Sons of Duke of York.*
RUTLAND.
WARWICK, LORD.—*First on the side of York, then of Lancaster.*
SOMERSET.
OXFORD. } *Lords of the Lancastrian Party.*
CLIFFORD.
TUTOR.—*To Rutland, young son of Duke of York.*
MARGARET OF ANJOU.—*Queen of Henry VI.*
ELIZABETH GREY.—*Queen of Edward IV.*
LADY BONA.—*Princess of France.*

EDWARD PLANTAGENET,

SON OF KING HENRY VI.

To this boy Shakespeare ascribes a manly spirit, worthy of his famous grandfather, Henry V, and of his heroic mother, Margaret of Anjou, a woman whom the old chronicle of Hall describes as "excelling all other, as well in beauty and favor as in wit and policy, and in courage more like to a man than a woman." But the child was unfortunate from his very birth. His father, at the time, was suffering from one of those attacks of insanity which at intervals clouded his life; the nobles were quarreling among themselves; the people were on the verge of rebellion.

The Duke of York had been made Protector during Henry's illness, and when Henry recovered he was not inclined to relinquish his power. Besides, he had a bitter quarrel with

the Duke of Somerset, who was a favorite ad-
viser and friend of King Henry and Queen
Margaret; and he had imprisoned him while
he was Protector. The King restored Somerset to all his old dignities, and the Duke of
York immediately raised an army to compel
Henry to dismiss Somerset from his councils
and deliver him up to justice. The great and
powerful Earl of Warwick espoused York's
quarrel, and Margaret, with all the warmth
and impetuosity of her nature, espoused the
cause of Somerset. To this rash interference
in the quarrel between York and Warwick
and Somerset, Philip de Comines, who knew
Margaret well, attributes all her misfortunes,
and the overthrow of the House of Lancaster.

Her whole life afterward was a weariful
watch and battle for the rights of her husband
and son; for Henry was indeed far more fit-
ted for a pope than a king, and his weak character and " bookish " rule " pulled fair England down." Then followed councils, quarrels,
treaties, and battles; and sometimes the King's
party had the victory, and sometimes the Duke
of York's. But at the battle of Northampton

the royal forces were completely routed, and
the King taken prisoner. In order to make
peace, Henry then disinherited his son, and
agreed that after his death the Duke of York
should be king.

In this scene (Scene I, Act I, Third Part
of Henry VI) it is impossible not to sympathize
with Margaret and her son; nor wonder, when
King Henry says

Be patient, gentle queen,

she should angrily reply--

Q. MAR. Who can be patient in such extremes?
Ah, wretched man! 'would I had died a maid,
And never seen thee, never borne thee son,
Seeing thou hast prov'd so unnatural a father!
Hath he deserved to lose his birthright thus?
Hadst thou but loved him half as well as I;
Or felt that pain which I did for him once;
Or nourish'd him, as I did with my blood;
Thou wouldst have left thy dearest heart-blood
        there,
Rather than have made that savage duke thine heir,
And disinherited thine only son.
PRINCE. Father, you can not disinherit me:
If you be king, why should not I succeed?

K. HEN. Pardon me, Margaret; pardon me, sweet
   son;
The earl of Warwick and the duke enforc'd me.
  Q. MAR. Enforc'd thee! Art thou king, and wilt
   be forced?
I shame to hear thee speak. Ah, timorous wretch!
Thou hast undone thyself, thy son, and me,
And given unto the house of York such head,
As thou shalt reign but by their sufferance.

   .   .   .   .

Had I been there, which am a silly woman,
The soldiers should have toss'd me on their pikes,
Before I would have granted to that act.

   .   .   .   .

The northern lords, that have forsworn thy colors,
Will follow mine, if once they see them spread;
And spread they shall be. . . .

                   Come, son, let's away;
Our army's ready; come, we'll after them.
  K. HEN. Stay, gentle Margaret, and hear me speak.
  Q. MAR. Thou hast spoke too much already; get
   thee gone.
  K. HEN. Gentle son Edward, thou wilt stay with
   me?
  Q. MAR. Ay, to be murder'd by his enemies.
  PRINCE. When I return with victory from the field
I'll see your grace: till then, I'll follow her.

The prince was then seven years of age;
he had been with his mother through several
campaigns; he knew what flight and exile
meant; he had witnessed the battles of Black-
heath and Northampton; and we can scarcely
wonder that, under the circumstances, he elect-
ed to follow his faithful and heroic mother.

In the next scene, while the Duke of York
and his two sons, Edward (afterward Edward
IV) and Richard (afterward Richard III) are
discussing the expediency of taking the crown,
without waiting for Henry's death, a messenger enters, and informs them that Margaret is
at hand with all the northern earls and lords,
and twenty thousand men. The battle which
ensued was a great victory for Margaret, but
it was sullied by the murder of "sweet young
Rutland," the little son of the Duke of York,
who was slain by Lord Clifford as he was flying with his tutor over Wakefield Bridge.

The sketch of this child is but a slight one,
but it is a masterly portrait of the terror and
eloquence of a boy who had been all his little
life under priestly dictation, who had a natural fear of death, and who could have no con-
ception of the scenes in which his Lancastrian

cousin Edward learned to defy his enemies, and receive their daggers without flinching.

RUT. Ah, whither shall I fly to 'scape their
    hands?
Ah, tutor! look where bloody Clifford comes!

Enter CLIFFORD *and* Soldiers.

CLIF. Chaplain, away! thy priesthood saves thy
    life.
As for the brat of this accursed duke,
Whose father slew my .father—he shall die.
    TUT. And I, my lord, will bear him company.
    CLIF. Soldiers, away with him.
    TUT. Ah, Clifford! murder not this innocent
    child,
Lest thou be hated both of God and man.
                [*Exit, forced off by* Soldiers.
    CLIF. How now! is he dead already? Or is it
    fear
That makes him close his eyes? I'll open them.
    RUT. So looks the pent-up lion o'er the wretch
That trembles under his devouring paws;
And so he walks, insulting o'er his prey,
And so he comes to rend his limbs asunder.
Ah, gentle Clifford, kill me with thy sword,
And not with such a cruel threat'ning look.

Sweet Clifford, hear me speak before I die;
I am too mean a subject for thy wrath;
Be thou reveng'd on men, and let me live.

CLIF. In vain thou speak'st, poor boy; my father's
blood
Hath stopp'd the passage where thy words should
enter.

RUT. Then let my father's blood open it again;
He is a man, and, Clifford, cope with him.

CLIF. Had I thy brethren here, their lives, and
thine,
Were not revenge sufficient for me;
No, if I digg'd up thy forefather's graves,
And hung their rotten coffins up in chains,
It could not slake mine ire, nor ease my heart.

.   .   .   .

Therefore—   [*Lifting his hand.*

RUT. O, let me pray before I take my death:
To thee I pray; sweet Clifford, pity me!

CLIF. Such pity as my rapier's point affords.

RUT. I never did thee harm: Why wilt thou slay
me?

CLIF. Thy father hath.

RUT.   But 'twas ere I was born.
Thou hast one son, for his sake pity me;
Lest, in revenge thereof—sith God is just—
He be as miserably slain as I.

Ah, let me live in prison all my days;
And when I give occasion of offense,
Then let me die, for now thou hast no cause.
   CLIF. No cause?
Thy father slew my father; therefore die.
                   [CLIFFORD *stabs him.*
   RUT. *Dii faciant laudis summa sit ista tuæ.*

In the next act Margaret presents the young
prince to his royal father for knighthood. The
boy was then in his eighth year, and he had
personally shared all the dangers and priva-
tions of the campaign.

   Q. MAR. My lord, cheer up your spirits;

   .   .   .   .

You promised knighthood to our forward son;
Unsheath your sword, and dub him presently.
Edward, kneel down.
   K. HEN. Edward Plantagenet, arise a knight;
And learn this lesson—Draw thy sword in right.
   PRINCE. My gracious father, by your kingly
        leave,
I'll draw it as apparent to the crown,
And in that quarrel use it to the death.

But this scene of exultation is quickly followed by the Lancastrian disaster on the field

of Towton—a disaster so great that the Prince
seeks out his father, and urges—

Fly, father, fly! for all our friends are fled,
And Warwick rages like a chafed bull.
Q. MAR. Mount you, my lord, toward Berwick
post amain:
Edward and Richard, like a brace of greyhounds
Having the fearful flying hare in sight,
With fiery eyes, sparkling for very wrath,
And bloody steel grasp'd in their ireful hands,
Are at our backs; and therefore hence amain.

This Yorkist victory firmly established Edward of York on the throne. King Henry was
imprisoned in the Tower, Margaret and the
prince fled to France. Then King Edward of
England makes proposals to marry the Lady
Bona, sister to the Queen of France, and Warwick is sent to France to arrange the matter
with Louis. But while Warwick is upon this
mission King Edward falls in love with the
Lady Elizabeth Grey, and marries her; which
so offends Warwick that he makes peace with
Margaret, and goes over to the interests of the
House of Lancaster.

In their behalf he quickly raises an army,

3

takes the crown from off King Edward's head,
and releases King Henry from his prison-cham-
ber in the Tower.   Then Edward flies to Belgia,
and, "with hasty Germans and blunt Holland-
ers" in his train, returns to England to fight
over again the battle for the crown.

In the mean time Margaret and her son
bring re-enforcements to Warwick from France;
but just before they land is fought the battle
of Barnet; and in it great Warwick is slain,
and Edward again victorious.   Even this terrible blow does not discourage the brave mother
and son.   On the plains near Tewkesbury they
have a conference with the Duke of Somerset
and the Earl of Oxford, and to them Margaret
says:

Great lords, wise men ne'er sit and wail their loss,
But cheerly seek how to redress their harms.
What, though the mast be now blown overboard,
The cable broke, the holding anchor lost,
And half our sailors swallowed in the flood?
Yet lives our pilot still:
    .   .   .   .

Why, is not Oxford here another anchor?
And Somerset another goodly mast?
The friends of France our shrouds and tacklings?

And, though unskillful, why not Ned and I
For once allowed the skillful pilot's charge?
We will not from the helm to sit and weep;
But keep our course, though the rough wind say no,
From shelves and rocks that threaten us with wreck.

.   .   .   .

Why, courage, then! what can not be avoided,
'Twere childish weakness to lament or fear.
PRINCE. Methinks a woman of this valiant spirit
Should, if a coward heard her speak these words,
Infuse his breast with magnanimity,
And make him, naked, foil a man at arms.
I speak not this as doubting any here:
For, did I but suspect a fearful man,
He should have leave to go away betimes;
Lest, in our need, he might infect another,
And make him of like spirit to himself.
If any such be here, as God forbid!
Let him depart, before we need his help!

OXF. Women and children of so high a courage,
And warriors faint! why, 'twere perpetual shame.
O, brave young prince! thy famous grandfather
Doth live again in thee; long may'st thou live
To bear his image, and renew his glories!

SOM. And he that will not fight for such a hope
Go home to bed, and, like the owl by day,
If he arise, be mock'd and wonder'd at.

Q. MAR. Thanks, gentle Somerset; sweet Oxford,
  thanks.

PRINCE. And take his thanks, that yet hath nothing else.

Then follows the battle of Tewkesbury, still
called "the bloody field." On it the last hopes
of the House of Lancaster were crushed with
the "gallant springing young Plantagenet."
Somerset, Oxford, Margaret, and Prince Edward,
are all taken prisoners, and brought into the
presence of King Edward, and his brothers
Clarence and Richard. King Edward orders
Oxford "to Hammes castle straight"; and
cries:

For Somerset, off with his guilty head.

Q. MAR. So part we sadly, in this troublous
  world,
To meet with joy in sweet Jerusalem.

K. EDW. Is proclamation made, that who finds
  Edward
Shall have a high reward, and he his life?

GLO. It is: and lo, where youthful Edward comes.
      [*Enter* Soldiers, *with* PRINCE EDWARD.

K. EDW. Bring forth the gallant, let us hear him
  speak:

What, can so young a thorn begin to prick?
Edward, what satisfaction canst thou make,
For bearing arms, for stirring up my subjects,
And all the trouble thou hast turn'd me to?

PRINCE. Speak like a subject, proud ambitious
    York!

Suppose that I am now my father's mouth;
Resign thy chair, and where I stand, kneel thou,
Whilst I propose the self-same words to thee,
Which, traitor, thou wouldst have me answer to.

Q. MAR. Ah, that thy father had been so resolv'd!

GLO. That you might still have worn the petti-
    coat,

And ne'er have stolen the breech from Lancaster.

PRINCE. Let Æsop fable in a winter's night;
His currish riddles sort not with this place.

GLO. By heaven, brat, I'll plague you for that
    word.

Q. MAR. Ay, thou wast born to be a plague to
    men.

GLO. For God's sake, take away this captive
    scold.

PRINCE. Nay, take away this scolding crook-back
    rather.

K. EDW. Peace, willful boy, or I will charm your
    tongue.

CLAR. Untutor'd lad, thou art too malapert.

PRINCE. I know my duty, you are all undutiful:
Lascivious Edward—and thou perjur'd George,*
And thou misshapen Dick, I tell ye all,
.I am your better, traitors as ye are:—
And thou usurp'st my father's right and mine.

K. EDW. Take that, the likeness of this railer here.
[*Stabs him.*

GLO. Sprawl'st thou? take that, to end thy agony.
[GLO. *stabs him.*

CLAR. And there's for twitting me with perjury.
[CLAR. *stabs him.*

Q. MAR. O, kill me too!

GLO. Marry, and shall.

K. EDW. Hold, Richard, hold, for we have done
too much.

GLO. Why should she live, to fill the world with
words?

K. EDW. What! doth she swoon? Use means
for her recovery.

GLO. Clarence, excuse me to the king my brother:
I'll hence to London on a serious matter;
Ere ye come there, be sure to hear some news.

CLAR. What? What?

GLO. The Tower, the Tower!

Q. MAR. O Ned, sweet Ned! speak to thy mother,
boy!

* George, Duke of Clarence.

Canst thou not speak?—O traitors! murderers!
They that stabb'd Cæsar shed no blood at all,
Did not offend, nor were not worthy blame,
If this foul deed were by, to equal it.
He was a man; this, in respect, a child;
And men ne'er spend their fury on a child.

.   .   .   .

Butchers and villains! bloody cannibals!
How sweet a plant have you untimely cropp'd!
You have no children, butchers! if you had,
The thought of them would have stirr'd up remorse:
But, if you ever chance to have a child,
Look in his youth to have him so cut off.
As, deathsmen! you have rid this sweet young
    prince!
  K. EDW. Away with her; go bear her hence per-
    force.
  Q. MAR. Nay, never bear me hence, dispatch me
    here;
Here sheathe thy sword, I'll pardon thee my death:
What! wilt thou not?—then, Clarence, do it thou.
  CLAR. By heaven, I will not do thee so much
    ease.
  Q. MAR. Good Clarence, do; sweet Clarence, do
    thou do it.
  CLAR. Didst thou not hear me swear I would not
    do it?

Q. MAR. Ay, but thou usest to forswear thyself;
'Twas sin before, but now 'tis charity.
What! wilt thou not? Where is the devil's butcher,
Hard-favored Richard? Richard, where art thou?
Thou art not here: Murder is thy alms-deed;
Petitioners for blood thou ne'er putt'st back.
> K. EDW. Away, I say; I charge ye, bear her hence.
> Q. MAR. So come to you, and yours, as to this
> prince!
> K. EDW. Where's Richard gone?
> CLAR. To London, all in post; and, as I guess,
To make a bloody supper in the Tower.

So fell this brave young prince, this noble
grandson of the great Henry V; a boy in
whom every personal and mental beauty were
united, but whose whole life was a stormy
scene of bloodshed and misfortune. Richard's
"bloody supper" in the Tower was the fitting
close to the cruel tragedy. He hastes to London, and, entering the room of the weak but
saintly Henry, he stabs him:

"O God! forgive my sins, and pardon thee!"

are the last words of the last king of the
House of Lancaster; while Richard mutters,
as he flings the dead body in another room:

King Henry, and the prince, his son, are gone:
Clarence, thy turn is next, and then the rest;
Counting myself but bad, till I be best.

Margaret's fate is announced at the close
of the play; for Clarence asks:

What will your grace have done with Margaret?
Reignier, her father, to the king of France
Hath pawn'd the Sicils and Jerusalem,
And hither have they sent it for her ransom.
    K. Edw. Away with her, and waft her hence to
        France.

EDWARD, SON OF HENRY VI.

THE war known in history as the "Wars of the Roses" covered the whole space of young Edward's life, and his history is inextricably united with it. But the bitterness and wrong which produced this war began long before the birth of Edward; in fact, England owed to the vices of King Richard II the civil war of King Henry VI.

Richard II inherited the throne through his father, the Black Prince, *eldest* son of King Edward III. But his weakness and wickedness stung his people into rebellion, and the crown was taken from him and given to Henry, son of the Duke of Lancaster, *fourth* son of Edward III. But, though Henry had gained the crown by his popularity, he had no inherited right to it; for, setting aside Richard altogether, the claim of the House of York came before that of the House of Lancaster, York being the *third*, and Lancaster the *fourth* son of the great Edward.

The House of Lancaster, however, being very wealthy and powerful, kept possession of the usurped scepter for three consecutive reigns —namely, that of Henry IV, who forcibly seized it, Henry V, his son, and Henry VI, his grandson—the three sovereigns who compose that branch of the Plantagenet dynasty which is called the Lancastrian.

But their sway was neither peaceful nor uncontested; and from the time that Henry VI ascended the throne, an infant but nine months old, the country was one continual scene of disorder and contention. Naturally weak and timid, possessed of every mild and endearing virtue, but totally deficient in every quality necessary to the ruler of a great nation, he became from his earliest childhood the tool of ambitious and designing guardians and ministers.

The measure of his misfortunes was completed by his marriage with Margaret of Anjou, a princess of singular beauty and accomplish-

ments, but of so masculine a spirit and so un-
yielding a temper that she increased the discontent felt toward Henry continually.

In the thirteenth year of his marriage with
Margaret, King Henry had a severe illness
which ended in imbecility of the most distress-
ing kind; then the long-smothered contentions
between the rival houses were openly re-
kindled, for the Duke of York, being next in
order to the throne, was made "protector and
defender of the realm" during the King's inca-
pacity.

At this critical juncture Edward Plantagenet
was born—"a child of infelicity and sorrow."
His birth gave little pleasure to the nation.
The distractions which had so long desolated
the kingdom were attributed, and most justly,
to the long minority of the King, and the pros-
pect of similar evils recurring in the person of
his son aroused a feeling of discontent, aggra-
vated by the imperious conduct of the Queen
and her favorite ministers—the Dukes of Suf-
folk and Somerset.

The power of the Duke of York was continually gaining ground; he governed well and
wisely, and, notwithstanding the birth of an

heir, the great mass of the people remembered still the prior right of his family to the throne. His first act was to consign the care of the King's person to Margaret, and enjoin her to withdraw with him and the infant prince to Hertford Castle. Margaret, however, soon returned to the palace at Greenwich, where she strengthened the Lancastrian party by holding frequent secret meetings with the princes and friends of the family.

When the little prince was in his sixth year she took him with the King in progress through the counties of Warwick, Stafford, and Cheshire, under pretense of benefiting his Majesty by change of air and sylvan sports. Her real object was to display the beauty of the young Prince of Wales, a child of singular promise, and she caused him to distribute little silver swans as his badge to all who pressed to look upon him. This was the device of his renowned ancestor, Edward III, whose name he bore; and so well were her impassioned pleadings in his behalf seconded by the loveliness and winning behavior of the little prince, that ten thousand men wore his livery at the subsequent battle of Blore-heath.

For matters now came to a bloody issue.
The Duke of York, irritated to extremity by
the personal and political opposition of the
Queen, appealed to Parliament for a recogni-
tion of his right and title to the throne; and
his claims, having been argued by the great
law-officers of the crown, were recognized by
the House of Lords. Reluctant to depose the
well-meaning, simple monarch, who was weak
both in body and mind, an act was passed to
the effect that Henry VI should retain the
scepter during his life, but that on his death
the succession should revert to the lawful heir,
the Duke of York.

The Queen was with the prince at Harlech,
in Wales, when this decision was communi-
cated to her; and she was ordered at once to
return to London with her son. The tidings
roused all the energies of her nature; the King
of Scotland was the son of a Lancastrian princess, and she fled to Scotland for assistance.
Here she was kindly entertained with the little
prince, and furnished with money and troops.
With these she crossed the Scottish border,
unfurled the banner of the Red Rose—the em-
blem of the House of Lancaster, as the White

Rose was of York—and, strengthened by all the chivalry of Northumberland, Cumberland, Lancaster, and Westmoreland, was at the gates of York before the leaders of the White Rose party knew that she was in England.

Here Margaret won a great victory, which she sullied by most unwomanly cruelty. The Duke of York and his kinsman, the Earl of Salisbury, were taken prisoners. York was dragged in mockery to an ant-hill, and insultingly placed there as on a throne; he was crowned with a diadem of knotted grass, while his enemies deridingly exclaimed: "Hail! king without a kingdom. Hail! prince without a people." His head was presented on a lance to the Queen, and by her command crowned with a paper crown and put over the gates of York, with the heads of Salisbury and other of his adherents. His second son, Rutland, a youth of singular beauty, flying from the fatal spot with his tutor, was overtaken by Lord Clifford, one of the friends of Margaret, and stabbed, even while praying for mercy.

But, though the Duke of York was slain, he left behind him three sons, Edward, Clarence, and Richard; and these three, goaded

to desperation by the bitter insults heaped
upon their murdered father, and the slaughter
of their young brother Rutland, united with an
energy and zeal nothing could resist.

After many desperate conflicts Henry and
Margaret, and their son Prince Edward, fled
again to Scotland; and Edward, the eldest son
of the murdered Duke of York, went to London, and by the title of Edward IV was
crowned king, thus becoming the founder of
the Yorkist dynasty — the Lancastrian King
Henry VI, Margaret, and even the boy prince,
being attainted by Parliament, and all subjects
forbidden to hold communication with them.

Then Margaret went to France, to solicit
from Louis XI—that man without a human
sympathy — the help she could find nowhere
else. She obtained some ships and men, and
attempted to land on the coast of Northumberland. But a panic seized her foreign troops,
and they fled, leaving Margaret and her boy
almost alone. A storm arose, and a fisherman's
boat received the royal fugitives, while the
French ships were dashed to pieces on the
rocky coast of Bamborough.

Hope must have been an undying faculty

in Margaret's heart. Once more she obtained
help in Scotland, brought King Henry from
his hiding-place in Wales, and for the first time
parted with her son ; for, not wishing to expose
his tender childhood to the hardships of a winter campaign, she left him with friends at Berwick. Her arms had only moderate success,
and in the spring, at the battle of Hexham, she
was completely defeated. At this battle the
prince was again by her side, and for some
time they wandered, cold and weary and hun-
gry, in the forest of Hexham. Here they were
plundered and threatened with death by some
robbers, but, a quarrel ensuing among them
concerning the sharing of the booty, they found
an opportunity to escape. This adventure was
succeeded by another apparently as perilous,
though it led them to shelter and security ; for,
when both were nearly fainting with fatigue
and hunger, they were again accosted by a
robber, who with drawn sword was about to
slay them, when Margaret put out her hand
and presented to him the young prince, saying : "Friend, use your sword in a better
cause ; I now commit to your care the son of
your king." The man, charmed with her cour-

age, and flattered by her confidence, secreted her in a hut in the forest, and finally arranged means of escape for her into Flanders.

Margaret was uncertain whether Henry was alive or dead, as they had fled in different directions; but it may be noticed here that she always, excepting the few months in which she sheltered him in Berwick, retained her son with her. They shared victory and defeat together. The child, from his earliest years, was used to cold and hunger and weariness, to the fatigue of flight and forced marches, to the sight of blood and battle.

Margaret was kindly received by the Duke of Burgundy; and her father gave her the castle of Kuerere, near the town of St. Michael, for her residence. Margaret now occupied herself in superintending the education of her son; and Sir John Fortescue, who was his tutor, wrote here, for the young prince's use, his celebrated work on the Constitution of England, *De Laudibus Legum Angliæ.*

In the mean time King Henry, who had fled from the battle of Hexham in a different direction from Margaret, fell into the hands of his enemies. At first he found refuge among the wilds of Westmoreland and Lancashire, and for many months was concealed in various castles and halls of these shires. But he was at length betrayed by a monk, and as he sat at dinner in Waddington Hall was taken prisoner by emissaries of Edward IV, his rival.

He was conducted to London in the most ignominious manner, with his legs fastened to the wretched nag on which he was mounted, and an insulting placard on his shoulders—a retaliation, doubtless, of Margaret's insults to the Duke of York, Edward IV's father. At Islington he was led thrice round the pillory, amid the jeers of the crowd; and one ruffian was base enough to strike him in the hour of his misery. "Forsooth, and forsooth; ye do foully to smite the Lord's anointed," was his mild rebuke.

Margaret and the gallant little prince felt this cruelty and indignity as the greatest aggravation of their own loss and trials. But the year 1469 saw the White Rose party divided against itself, and the throne of Edward IV tottering. Margaret and Prince Edward immediately had a meeting with Louis of France and other friends in order to consider on the best way of improving the crisis for the House of Lancaster. Margaret was in a fever of hope. The northern and midland counties were in arms against King Edward, led by the Duke of Warwick; and in a few months Edward was taken prisoner and sent to the stronghold of Middleham Castle, under the wardship of Warwick's brother, the Archbishop of York. So England had at this time two kings, and both of them in prison.

Edward, however, escaped, gathered an army, and compelled Warwick to fly to France. Here he had an interview with Margaret and her son, and offered to unite his immense power and influence to the House of Lancaster; and, to cement the union, a marriage was arranged between Warwick's daughter, Anne, and the boy prince, Edward.

Then Warwick returned to England, landed at Dartmouth, and proclaimed his intention of delivering King Henry from prison, declaring his commission to be "by the whole voice and assent of the most noble Princess Margaret, Queen of England, and the right high and mighty Prince Edward." Warwick found himself in a few days at the head of sixty thousand men, the people crying everywhere: "A Henry! A Henry!"

Again Edward IV was obliged to fly to Holland, and Warwick sent the Bishop of Winchester to the Tower of London, to take King Henry VI from his keepers, and " bring him home to his palace at Westminster with great reverence and rejoicing."

Margaret and Prince Edward immediately made preparations to return to England. But an evil fate persistently pursued this unfortunate woman. They landed almost at the very time when the Lancastrian cause was receiving its death-blow on the fatal heath of Barnet. Here Warwick was slain, and King Henry again taken prisoner. When the news was brought to them, Margaret fainted away; but the prince "soothed and caressed her with many hopeful and courageous words," and she sought, with all her company, the famous sanctuary of Beaulieu Abbey.

Here they were soon visited by the fiery young Duke of Somerset, and many other Lancastrian nobles; and they said "they had already a good puissance in the field, and with her presence, and that of the prince, would

soon draw all the northern and western counties to the banner of the Red Rose." Margaret wished, however, to return to France; but
"the gallant young prince would not consent
to this; both Somerset and he were determined still to keep war against their enemies."
So the whole party proceeded with this escort
of Lancastrian lords to Bath.

It was a peculiarity in Margaret's campaigns
that she always kept the place of her destina-
tion a profound secret. Owing to this caution,
and the entire devotion of the western counties to her cause, she had a large army in the
field ready to oppose Edward IV, while her
actual locality remained unknown to him. Edward advanced to Marlborough; Margaret and
Prince Edward retreated to Bristol, intending
to cross the Severn and make a junction with
Jaspar Tudor's army in Wales. Could this
have been effected, there might have been a
different tale to tell than that of the bloody,
dismal day of Tewkesbury; but the men of
Gloucester had fortified the bridge, and would
not let her cross, either for threats or bribes.

Margaret and Prince Edward then passed
on to Tewkesbury. Edward was waiting for

them. They had marched thirty-seven miles that day. Somerset led the advanced guard, the Prince of Wales commanded the van, the Earl of Devonshire the rearward. When the battle was in order, Margaret and the prince rode from rank to rank encouraging the men, and promising large rewards if victory was won.

The battle was fought, and lost, on May 4, 1471. There Margaret saw the last hopes of Lancaster crushed with her "gallant springing young Plantagenet." The following graphic account of his death is from the chronicle of Hall:

"After the field ended King Edward made a proclamation that whosoever could bring Prince Edward to him, alive or dead, should have an annuity during his life, and the prince's life to be saved. Sir Richard Croftes, a wise and a valiant knight, nothing mistrusting the King's former promise, brought forth his prisoner, Prince Edward, being a goodly and well-featured young gentleman, whom, when King Edward had well advised, he demanded of him how he durst so presumptuously enter into his realm with banner displayed. The prince, being bold of stomach, and of a good courage, answered, saying: 'To recover my father's kingdom and heritage from his father and grandfather to him.' At which words King Edward said nothing, but with his hand thrust him from him—or, as some say, struck him with his gauntlet—whom incontinent they that strode about, which were George, Duke of Clarence, Richard, Duke of Gloster, Thomas Marquis Dorset, and William Lord Hastings, suddenly murdered, and piteously mangled. His body was homely interred with other simple corpses in the Church of the Monastery of Black Monks in Tewkesbury."

The following day the news of her son's death was taken to Margaret by her old enemy, Sir William Stanley, and revealed to her in a manner so brutal as to aggravate greatly the bitterness of the blow. Margaret invoked the most terrible maledictions on her son's murderers and on Edward and his sons, which hasty passionate words Stanley inhumanly repeated to Edward. At first Edward thought of putting her to death; but no Plantagenet had ever shed the blood of a woman, and, after forcing her to grace his triumph to London, he incarcerated her in one of the most dismal lodgings of the gloomy Tower.

The same night that Margaret was taken to the Tower she was made a widow. "That night," says Leland, "between eleven and twelve of the clock, was King Henry, being prisoner in the Tower, put to death, the Duke of Gloster, and divers of his men, being in the Tower that night." Tradition points out an octagonal room in the Wakefield Tower as the scene of the midnight murder of Henry VI. It was there that he had for five years eat the bread of his sad and lonely affliction, a few learned manuscripts and devotional books, and a little bird, his only companions.

The imprisonment of Margaret was at first very rigorous, but she was finally ransomed by her tender-hearted father — the famous King René — by the sacrifice of his inheritance of Provence, which he ceded to Louis XI for half its value, in order to deliver his beloved child from captivity.

There is something very touching in the deed which was wrung from the broken-hearted woman who had so long defended the rights of her husband and son. While they lived she

4

would rather have given up her life than have
relinquished a claim they possessed; but, when
they were gone,

> "Ambition, pride, the rival names
>   Of York and Lancaster,
>   With all their long-contested claims—
>   What were they then to her?"

Almost as a matter of indifference she signed
the instrument—" I, Margaret, formerly in England married, renounce all that I could pretend
to in England by the conditions of my marriage, with all other things there, to Edward,
now King of England." And thus for ever terminated a dispute which for twenty years had
filled the land with distraction and loss and
slaughter.

The poetic badges of this bloody civil war
are accounted for by Shakespeare in a splendid
scene in the Temple Gardens (First Part of
King Henry VI, Act II, Scene 4), in which
lords of the rival houses pluck red and white
roses as their emblems. But these emblems
were used long before the reign of Henry VI
as cognizances of the two dukedoms; the badges
were then only revived, not adopted. Edmund,

Earl of Lancaster, the brother of Edward I, has red roses emblazoned on his tomb; and Edward the Black Prince wears a coronet of white roses in the portrait of him, which is preserved in Richard II's missal, now in the Harleian Collection.

EDWARD V, AND RICHARD, DUKE OF YORK,

SONS OF KING EDWARD IV.

PERSONS IN THE DRAMA.

EDWARD.—*King of England.*

EDWARD V.
RICHARD, DUKE OF YORK. } *His Sons.*

GEORGE, DUKE OF CLARENCE.
RICHARD, DUKE OF GLOSTER. } *The King's Brothers.*

DUKE OF RICHMOND.—*Afterward* HENRY VII.

HASTINGS.
BUCKINGHAM.
RIVERS.
GREY. } *English Lords.*

SIR ROBERT BRAKENBURY.—*Lieutenant of the Tower.*

SIR JAMES TYRREL.—*A Creature of Gloster's.*

SON AND DAUGHTER OF CLARENCE.

ELIZABETH.—*Queen of Edward IV.*

DUCHESS OF YORK.—*Mother of Edward IV, Clarence, and Richard.*

ANNE.—*Wife to Richard of Gloster.*

EDWARD V, AND RICHARD, DUKE OF YORK,

SONS OF KING EDWARD IV.

THE play of "Richard III," which follows that of "King Henry VI," is its necessary sequel. Edward IV is now undisputed King of England; for, after the murder of Henry VI and his son Edward, all the heirs of Edward III, excepting those of the House of York, were dead. But though the civil war was over, it was followed by a domestic one in the reigning family, which turned the royal palace into a slaughter-house.

The three York brothers—King Edward VI, George, Duke of Clarence, and Richard, Duke of Gloster—feared each other; and Clarence, doubted by Edward, and standing between Richard and the throne, fell first. In that "miserable night" before his murder, "so full of

fearful dreams, of ugly sights," and "dismal terror," Clarence tells, shudderingly, how among
them there

Came wandering by
A shadow like an angel, with bright hair
Dabbled in blood, and he shriek'd out aloud—
Clarence is come—false, fleeting, perjur'd Clarence,
That stabb'd me in the field by Tewkesbury,
Seize on him, furies, take him to your torments!

In the next act, one of the first scenes shows
us the mother and children of the murdered
Clarence. The little son of Clarence is a very
pretty picture of an innocent, credulous child.
His uncle Gloster has been at some trouble
to deceive him; he has kissed and petted and
pitied him, and the boy will not believe there
is any guile beneath these kind appearances.

SCENE II.

Enter the DUCHESS OF YORK *with a* SON *and* DAUGH-
TER *of* CLARENCE.

SON. Good grandam, tell us, is our father dead?
DUCH. No, boy.
DAUGH. Why do you weep so oft? and beat your
breast;
And cry—*O Clarence, my unhappy son!*

SON. Why do you look on us and shake your head,
And call us—orphans, wretches, castaways,
If that our noble father be alive?

DUCH. My pretty cousins, you mistake me both;
I do lament the sickness of the king,
As loath to lose him, not your father's death:
It were lost sorrow to wail one that's lost.

SON. Then, grandam, you conclude that he is dead.
The king my uncle is to blame for this:
God will revenge it; whom I will importune
With earnest prayers all to that effect.

DAUGH. And so will I.

DUCH. Peace, children, peace! the king doth love
    you well:
Incapable and shallow innocents,
You can not guess who caus'd your father's death.

SON. Grandam, we can; for my good uncle Glos-
    ter
Told me the king, provok'd to 't by the queen,
Devised impeachments to imprison him:
And when my uncle told me so, he wept,
And pitied me, and kindly kiss'd my cheek;
Bade me rely on him, as on my father,
And he would love me dearly as his child.

DUCH. Ah, that deceit should steal such gentle
    shape.

Son. Think you my uncle did dissemble, grandam?

Duch. Ay, boy.

Son. I can not think it.

Their sorrowful conversation is interrupted
by the distracted lamentation of Queen Elizabeth for the death of her husband, Edward IV,
whose decease follows hard on the murder of
his brother Clarence. Then Lord Rivers advises her—

Madam, bethink you, like a careful mother,
Of the young prince your son: send straight for
him,
Let him be crowned: in him your comfort lives.

The young Prince of Wales was then thir-
teen years of age and at Ludlow, the ancient
home of the Princes of Wales. His brother
Richard, the young Duke of York, was eleven,
and was with his mother and grandmother in
the palace. These two boys Shakespeare has
drawn with exquisite skill; the elder, Edward,
is dignified, earnest, and clear-seeing; the
younger, Richard, is quick, keen, intelligent, and
a lively observer of persons and things.

We see him first in a room of the palace anxiously waiting with his grandmother and mother the arrival of his brother from Ludlow. The Archbishop of York enters, and tells them—

Last night, I heard, they lay at Stony-Stratford;
And at Northampton they do rest to-night:
To-morrow, or next day, they will be here.

DUCH. I long with all my heart to see the prince;
I hope he is much grown since last I saw him.

Q. ELIZ. But I hear, no; they say my son of York
Hath almost overta'en him in his growth.

YORK. Ay, mother, but I would not have it so.

DUCH. Why, my young cousin? it is good to grow.

YORK. Grandam, one night, as we did sit at supper,
My uncle Rivers talk'd how I did grow
More than my brother; *Ay*, quoth my uncle Gloster,
Small herbs have grace, great weeds do grow apace:
And since, methinks, I would not grow so fast,
Because sweet flowers are slow, and weeds make haste.

DUCH. 'Good faith, 'good faith, the saying did not hold

In him that did object the same to thee:
He was the wretched'st thing, when he was young:
So long a growing, and so leisurely,
That, if his rule were true, he should be gracious.

   .   .   .   .

 York. Now, by my troth, if I had been remember'd,
I could have given my uncle's grace a flout,
To touch his growth, nearer than he touch'd mine.
 Duch. How, my young York? I pr'ythee let me
  hear it.
 York. Marry, they say, my uncle grew so fast
That he could gnaw a crust at two hours old;
'Twas full two years ere I could get a tooth.
Grandam, this would have been a biting jest.
 Duch. I pr'ythee, pretty York, who told thee
  this?
 York. Grandam, his nurse.
 Duch. His nurse? why, she was dead ere thou
  wast born.
 York. If 'twere not she, I can not tell who told
  me.
 Q. Eliz. A parlous boy: Go to, you are too
  shrewd.
 Arch. Good madam, be not angry with the
  child.
 Q. Eliz. Pitchers have ears.

Edward V's Entry into London.

Edward V, and Richard, Duke of York.

But even before the Prince of Wales—now Edward V — arrives his mother has become alarmed, and fled to Sanctuary with her youngest son. Her brother, the Earl of Rivers, has been sent to prison by Gloster, and the mother-heart of the poor queen divines that this is but the beginning of the end. So, when the little king arrives in London, he misses at once his maternal uncle, and says to Gloster—

> I want more uncles here to welcome me.
> GLO. Sweet prince, the untainted virtue of your
>   years
> Hath not yet div'd into the world's deceit:
> .   .   .   .   .   .
> Those uncles, which you want, were dangerous;
> Your grace attended to their sugar'd words,
> But look'd not on the poison of their hearts:
> God keep you from them, and from such false
>   friends!
> PRINCE. God keep me from false friends! but
>   they were none.
> .   .   .   .
> I thought my mother, and my brother York,
> Would long ere this have met us on the way.

Then Lord Hastings enters, and informs him—

The queen your mother, and your brother York,
Have taken sanctuary: The tender prince
Would fain have come with me to meet your grace,
But by his mother was perforce withheld.

Buckingham, a creature of Gloster's, then desires Hastings to return to the Queen and persuade her to "send the Duke of York unto his princely brother presently; if she deny, from her jealous arms pluck him perforce."

PRINCE. Good lords, make all the speedy haste
   you may.
Say, uncle Gloster, if our brother come,
Where shall we sojourn till our coronation?
GLO. Where it seems best unto your royal self.
If I may counsel you, some day, or two,
Your highness shall repose you at the Tower:
Then where you please, and shall be thought most fit
For your best health and recreation.
PRINCE. I do not like the Tower, of any place:—
Did Julius Cæsar build that place, my lord?
GLO. He did, my gracious lord, begin that place;
Which, since, succeeding ages have re-edified.
PRINCE. Is it upon record? or else reported
Successively from age to age, he built it?
BUCK. Upon record, my gracious lord.

PRINCE. But say, my lord, it were not regis-
    ter'd;
Methinks, the truth should live from age to age,
As 'twere retail'd to all posterity,
Even to the general all-ending day.

   .   .   .   .   .

That Julius Cæsar was a famous man;
With what his valor did enrich his wit,
His wit set down to make his valor live.
Death makes no conquest of this conqueror;
For now he lives in fame, though not in life.
I'll tell you what my cousin Buckingham.
  BUCK. What, my gracious lord?
  PRINCE. An if I live until I be a man,
I'll win our ancient right in France again,
Or die a soldier, as I lived a king.
  GLO. Short summers lightly have a forward spring.
    [*Aside.*

In the ensuing meeting between the brothers, they are very finely contrasted. The young
Duke of York is bold, precocious, and inclined
to a boyish sauciness; and evidently discerns
the danger he has neither the power to ward
off nor the wisdom to ignore. On the contrary, a sweet and tender gravity blends with
everything the little king says. How much

feeling and modesty there are in his reflection on his father's death! and in the censuring question to his brother, what a delicate reminder of propriety! In his reply to Gloster, referring to his dead uncles, what caution and acuteness are shown by the equivocal words! Indeed, the whole scene indicates a disposition promising the most perfect manhood.

BUCK. Now, in good time, here comes the Duke of York.

PRINCE. Richard of York! how fares our loving brother?

YORK. Well, my dread lord; so must I call you now.

PRINCE. Ay, brother; to our grief, as it is yours;
Too late he died that might have kept that title,
Which by his death hath lost much majesty.

GLO. How fares our cousin, noble lord of York?

YORK. I thank you, gentle uncle.   O, my lord,
You said that idle weeds are fast in growth:
The prince my brother hath outgrown me far.

GLO. He hath, my lord.

YORK.   And therefore is he idle?

GLO. O, my fair cousin, I must not say so.

YORK. Then is he more beholden to you than I.

GLO. He may command me, as my sovereign;
But you have power in me, as in a kinsman.

YORK. I pray you, uncle, give me this dagger.

GLO. My dagger, little cousin? With all my heart.

PRINCE. A beggar, brother?

YORK. Of my kind uncle, that I know will give;
And, being but a toy, which is no grief to give.

GLO. A greater gift than that I'll give my cousin.

YORK. A greater gift! O, that's the sword to it?

GLO. Ay, gentle cousin, were it light enough.

YORK. O, then, I see, you'll part but with light
 gifts :

In weightier things you'll say a beggar, nay.

GLO. It is too weighty for your grace to wear.

YORK. I weigh it lightly, were it heavier.

GLO. What, would you have my weapon, little
 lord?

YORK. I would, that I might thank you as you
 call me.

GLO. How?

YORK. Little.

PRINCE. My lord of York will still be cross in
 talk ;—

Uncle, your grace knows how to bear with him.

YORK. You mean, to bear me, not to bear with
 me :—

Uncle, my brother mocks both you and me ;

Because that I am little, like an ape,

He thinks that you should bear me on your shoulders.

Buck. With what a sharp-provided wit he reasons!
To mitigate the scorn he gives his uncle,
He prettily and aptly taunts himself:
So cunning, and so young, is wonderful.
    Glo. My gracious lord, will it please you pass
        along?
Myself, and my good cousin Buckingham,
Will to your mother; to entreat of her
To meet you at the Tower, and welcome you.
    York. What, will you go unto the Tower, my lord?
    Prince. My lord protector needs will have it so.
    York. I shall not sleep in quiet at the Tower.
    Glo. Why, what should you fear?
    York. Marry, my uncle Clarence's angry ghost;
My grandam told me he was murder'd there.
    Prince. I fear no uncles dead.
    Glo. Nor none that live, I hope.
    Prince. An if they live, I hope, I need not fear.
But come, my lord, and, with a heavy heart,
Thinking on them, go I unto the Tower.

The short conversation which ensues, on the departure of the princes, between Gloster and Buckingham, well indicates their true feelings toward the doomed children:

    Buck. Think, you, my lord, this little prating
    York

Was not incensed by his subtle mother
To taunt and scorn you thus opprobriously?
  GLO. No doubt, no doubt; O, 'tis a parlous
    boy;
Bold, quick, ingenious, forward, capable;
He's all the mother's, from the top to toe.

Then follows the execution of Rivers, Grey,
Hastings—nobles likely to interfere with Richard's scheme for making himself king; and,
through Buckingham's assistance, the mayor
and citizens are finally induced to offer Gloster the crown, which he accepts, after a great
deal of pretended reluctance, saying:

Cousin of Buckingham—and you sage, grave men—
Since you will buckle fortune on my back,
To bear her burden, whe'r I will, or no,
I must have patience to endure the load.

The first result of this usurpation is an order confining the princes closely to the Tower,
and forbidding their mother and friends to visit
them. Act Fourth opens with a meeting of
Queen Elizabeth and their grandmother and
aunt before the Tower, and the refusal of
the lieutenant, Sir Robert Brakenbury, to ad-
mit them.

BRAK.   .... By your patience,
I may not suffer you to visit them;
The king hath strictly charg'd the contrary.

  Q. ELIZ. The king! Who's that?

  BRAK.   I mean, the lord protector.

  Q. ELIZ. The Lord protect him from that kingly
     title!
Hath he set bounds between their love and me?
I am their mother: who shall bar me from them?

  DUCH. I am their father's mother; I will see them.

  ANNE. Their aunt I am in law, in love their
     mother;
Then bring me to their sights; I'll bear thy blame,
And take thy office from thee, on my peril.

  BRAK. No, madam, no, I may not leave it so;
I am bound by oath, and therefore pardon me.

How sad and woful were the presenti-
ments of these wretched women is shown by
the aged grandmother urging the boys' mother
to seek her own safety. "Go thou to Sanctuary," she says.

Go thou to Sanctuary, and good thoughts possess thee!
I, to my grave, where peace and rest lie with me!
Eighty odd years of sorrow have I seen,
And each hour's joy wreck'd with a week of teen.

Q. ELIZ. Stay yet; look back, with me, unto the
  Tower.—
Pity, yon ancient stones, those tender babes,
Whom envy hath immur'd within your walls!
Rough cradle for such little pretty ones!
Rude ragged nurse! old sullen playfellow
For tender princes, use my babies well!

Buckingham, who had not feared to follow
all Gloster's bloody ways, so far, hesitates,
however, when Gloster suggests the murder of
his nephews. " Give me some breath," he asks,

    —some little pause, dear lord,
Before I positively speak in this.

Then King Richard, telling himself disdain-
fully that " High-reaching Buckingham grows
circumspect," calls a page, and asks him if he
knows any one " whom corrupting gold

Would tempt into a close exploit of death?"

The page suggests Sir James Tyrrel, "a
discontented gentleman, whose humble means
match not his haughty mind."

K. RICH. I partly know the man; Go, call him
  hither, boy—

 . . . .

Is thy name Tyrrel?

TYR. James Tyrrel, and your most obedient subject.

K. RICH. Art thou indeed?

TYR.   Prove me, my gracious lord.

K. RICH. Dar'st thou resolve to kill a friend of
mine?

TYR. Please you; but I had rather kill two enemies.

K. RICH. Why, then thou hast it; two deep enemies,

Foes to my rest, and my sweet sleep's disturbers,
Are they that I would have thee deal upon:
Tyrrel, I mean those bastards in the Tower.

TYR. Let me have open means to come to them,
And soon I'll rid you from the fear of them.

K. RICH. Thou sing'st sweet music. Hark, come
hither, Tyrrel;

Go, by this token:—Rise, and lend thine ear:

[*Whispers.*

There is no more but so; say, it is done,
And I will love thee, and prefer thee for it.

TYR. I will dispatch it straight.

The consummation of this bloody tragedy
Tyrrel tells himself in the Third Scene of the
Fourth Act.

The Princes in the Tower.

Edward V, and Richard, Duke of York.

Enter TYRREL.

TYR. The tyrannous and bloody act is done;
The most arch deed of piteous massacre
That ever yet this land was guilty of.
Dighton, and Forrest, whom I did suborn
To do this piece of ruthless butchery,
Albeit they were flesh'd villains, bloody dogs,
Melting with tenderness and mild compassion,
Wept like two children, in their death's sad story.
O thus, quoth Dighton, *lay the gentle babes,—*
Thus, thus, quoth Forrest, *girdling one another*
Within their alabaster innocent arms:
Their lips were four red roses on a stalk,
Which, in their summer beauty, kiss'd each other.
A book of prayers on their pillow lay;
Which once, quoth Forrest, *almost chang'd my mind;*
But, O, the devil—there the villain stopp'd:
When Dighton thus told on—*we smothered*
The most replenished sweet work of Nature,
That, from the prime creation, e'er she fram'd.—
Hence both are gone with conscience and remorse;
They could not speak; and so I left them both,
To bear this tidings to the bloody king.

Enter KING RICHARD.

And here he comes:—All health, my soverign lord!
K. RICH. Kind Tyrrel! am I happy in thy news?

TYR. If to have done the thing you gave in
 charge
Beget your happiness, be happy then,
For it is done.
 K. RICH. But didst thou see them dead?
 TYR. I did, my lord. .
 K. RICH.   And buried, gentle Tyrrel?
 TYR. The chaplain of the Tower hath buried
 them;
But where, to say the truth, I do not know.
 K. RICH. Come to me, Tyrrel, soon, at after sup-
 per,
When thou shalt tell the process of their death.
Meantime, but think how I may do thee good
And be inheritor of thy desire.
Farewell, till then.
 TYR.   I humbly take my leave.
 K. RICH. The son of Clarence have I penn'd up
 close;
His daughter meanly have I match'd in marriage;
The sons of Edward sleep in Abraham's bosom,
And Anne my wife hath bid the world good
 night.
Now, for I know the Bretagne Richmond aims
At young Elizabeth, my brother's daughter,
And, by that knot, looks proudly on the crown,
To her go I, a jolly, thriving wooer.

But even while he speaks a messenger enters, bringing tidings that his old ally Buckingham is fled to Richmond, with whom are also Dorset, Morton, and a host of other powerful confederates. Indeed, he soon finds that he has no friends left but those "who are friends for fear"; for "every man's conscience is a thousand swords, to fight against that bloody homicide."

The armies of Richard and Richmond meet for one decisive battle on the field of Bosworth; but, at the midnight before the fatal day, Richard receives awful assurance of the death and disaster awaiting him. First the ghost of Prince Edward, son of Henry VI, comes to him and says:

Let me sit heavy on thy soul to-morrow!
Think how thou stabb'dst me in my prime of youth
At Tewkesbury; Despair, therefore, and die!

Then the ghost of Henry VI appears, saying:

When I was mortal, my anointed body
By thee was punched full of deadly holes:
Think on the Tower, and me; Despair, and die!
Henry VI bids thee despair and die.

5

The Ghost *of* Clarence *rises.*

Ghost. Let me sit heavy on thy soul to-morrow!
I, that was wash'd to death with fulsome wine,
Poor Clarence, by thy guile betray'd to death!
To-morrow in the battle think of me,
And fall thy edgeless sword; Despair, and die!

.   .   .   .

Ghosts *of the two young* Princes *rise.*

Ghosts. Dream on thy cousins smothered in the
    Tower;
Let us be lead within thy bosom, Richard,
And weigh thee down to ruin, shame, and death!
Thy nephews' souls bid thee despair, and die.

The ghosts of his murdered queen, Anne,
and of his friend Buckingham, fill up the awful measure of a denunciation which makes
even Richard's conscience cry out—

Guilty! Guilty!
I shall despair.—There is no creature loves me!
And, if I die, no soul will pity me.

Within a few hours Richard falls, fighting
desperately, on Bosworth field; and the kind
of pity he anticipated is all that he receives—

". . . . the bloody dog is dead."

HISTORICAL SKETCH

OF

EDWARD AND RICHARD PLANTAGENET,
SONS OF KING EDWARD IV.

It was in the very darkest hour of the last struggle of the House of York for the crown of England that Edward Plantagenet, son of Edward IV, was born. Warwick, after his reconciliation with the House of Lancaster, had just entered London, Edward the King had fled to Holland, and Queen Elizabeth, with her three daughters, had taken refuge in a strong gloomy building called the Sanctuary, which stood at the end of St. Margaret's churchyard.

Here, on the 1st of November, A. D. 1470, the long-hoped-for heir of York was born. "Never before had Westminster Sanctuary received a royal guest, and little was it ever deemed a Prince of Wales would first see light within walls that had hitherto only sheltered homicides, robbers, and bankrupts. But the revolution for Edward's restoration was as rapid as that of his deposition. On Easter Sunday Edward gained the battle of Barnet, in which Warwick was killed; and then Elizabeth retired to the Tower until her husband on the field of Tewkesbury put down for ever the hopes of the House of Lancaster.

The little Richard, Duke of York, was born, about two years after his brother, at Shrewsbury, 1472, and the earliest event of importance in his short life was his marriage with Anne Mowbray, the infant heiress of the duchy of Norfolk. St. Stephen's Chapel, where the ceremony was performed, January, A. D. 1477, was splendidly hung with arras of gold on this occasion. The King, the young Prince of Wales, and the three princesses, Elizabeth, Mary, and Cicely, were present; the Queen led the little bridegroom, who was not five years old, and her brother, Earl Rivers, led the baby bride, scarcely three years old. The innocent and ill-fated infants then married verified the old English proverb, which says,·

"Early wed, early dead."

King Edward IV died at Westminster April
9, 1483, the Prince of Wales being then in his
thirteenth year. He was at Ludlow Castle pre-
siding over his principality of Wales, and pur-
suing his studies under the care of his accomplished uncle Rivers. Elizabeth sat at the first
council after the death of her husband, and
proposed that the young king should be es-
corted to London with a powerful army. Hastings, prompted by jealousy of the Queen's family, contradicted this prudent measure, asking,
insolently, " against whom the young sovereign was to be defended? Who were his foes?
Not his valiant uncle, Gloster! Not Stanley,
or himself!" He finished by vowing " that
he would retire from court if the young king
was brought to London surrounded by soldiers."

Elizabeth gave up her precaution with tears;
and her maternal forebodings received only too
sad confirmation when, at midnight, on the 3d
of May, tidings were brought her that the Duke
of Gloster had intercepted the young king with
an armed force. In that hour of agony she
however remembered that, while she could
keep her second son in safety, the life of the

young king was secure. " Therefore," says Hall, "she took her young son, the Duke of York, and her daughters, and went out of the palace of Westminster into the Sanctuary, and there lodged in the Abbot's place; and she and all her children and company were registered as Sanctuary persons."

The apartments of the Abbot of Westminster are nearly in the same state, at the present hour, as when they received Elizabeth and her train of young princesses. The noble hall, now used as a dining-room for students of Westminster School, was, doubtless, the place where Elizabeth seated herself in her despair, as the old chronicle says, " *alow* on the rushes, all desolate and dismayed." The Princess Mary had died a year before, but Elizabeth took into Sanctuary with her the Duke of York, aged eleven; the Princesses Elizabeth, aged seventeen; Cicely, aged fifteen; Anne, aged eight; Katherine, aged four; and a babe called Bridget.

The 4th of May had been appointed for the young king's coronation, but his false uncle did not bring him to London until that day. Then Edward V entered the city surrounded by officers of the Duke of Gloster's retinue. At the head of the *posse* rode Gloster himself, habited in black, with his cap in his hand, " ofttimes bowing low, and pointing out his nephew (who wore the royal mantle of purple velvet) to the homage of the citizens."

At first Edward V was lodged with the Bishop of Ely, but Gloster soon had him transferred to the regal apartments in the Tower. His next object was to get possession of his brother, the Prince Richard; and, after a long and stormy debate in council, it was decided that, " as children could commit no crime for which an asylum was needed, the privileges of Sanctuary could not extend to them, therefore, the Duke of Gloster, who was now recognized as lord protector, could possess himself of his nephew by force, if he pleased."

The Archbishop of Canterbury was unwilling that force should be used, and he went with a deputation of temporal peers to persuade Elizabeth to surrender her son. Very sorrowfully she delivered the poor child, saying: " These children are safe while they be asunder. Notwithstanding, I here deliver him, and his brother's life with him, into your hands; and of you I shall require them before God and man." Then, drawing the child to her, she said: "Farewell! mine own sweet son! God send you good keeping! Let me kiss you once ere you go, for God knoweth when we shall kiss together again!" And therewith "she kissed and blessed him, and turned her back and wept, leaving the poor, innocent child weeping as fast as herself." "Then," says Sir Thomas More, "they brought the young duke into the star-chamber, where the lord protector took him in his arms with these words: 'Now welcome, my lord, with all my very heart!' He then brought him to the bishop's palace at St. Paul's, and from thence honorably through the city to the young king at the Tower, out of which they were never seen abroad."

Among the gloomy range of fortresses belonging to the Tower, tradition points out the Portcullis tower as the scene of the murder of the young princes. "Forthwith," says Sir Thomas More, "they were both shut up, and all their people removed but only one, called Black·Will, or Will Slaughter, who was set to serve them, and four keepers to guard them.

The young king was heard to say, sighingly, 'I would mine uncle would let me have my life, though he taketh my crown.' After which time the prince never tied his points, nor anything attended to himself, but with that young babe, his brother, lingered in thought and heaviness till the traitorous deed delivered them from wretchedness."

During Richard's progress to the North in September, 1484—the September following the young Edward V's entry into London in May—Richard one night roused Sir James Tyrrel from his pallet-bed in his guard-chamber and ordered him to go to London and destroy the royal children. Sir Robert Brakenbury refused to co-operate, but he gave up the keys of the Tower for one night to Tyrrel.

"Then Sir James Tyrrel devised that the princes should be murdered in bed; to the execution thereof he appropriated Miles Forest, one of their keepers, a fellow bred in murder; and to him he joined one John Dighton, his own horse-keeper, a big, broad, square knave. All their other attendants being removed from them, and the harmless children in bed, these men came into their chamber, and suddenly lapping them in the clothes, smothered and stifled them till thoroughly dead; then laying out their bodies in the bed, they fetched Sir James to see them, who caused the murderers to bury them at the stair foot, deep in the ground, under a heap of stones.

"But when the news was first brought to the unfortunate mother, yet being in Sanctuary, that her two sons were murdered, it struck to her heart like the sharp dart of death; she swooned and fell to the ground, and there lay in great agony, yet like to a dead corpse. And after she was revived and come to her memory again she wept and sobbed, and with pitiful screeches filled the whole mansion. Her breast she beat, her fair hair she tore, and calling by name her sweet babes, accounted herself mad when she delivered her younger son out of Sanctuary for his uncle to put him to death, . . . and when in a few months Richard unexpectedly lost his only son, the child for whose advancement he had steeped his soul in crime, Englishmen declared that the cries of the agonized mother to God for vengeance had been heard."

Tyrrel, the instigator of the murder, was

condemned for some minor Yorkist plot as late
as A. D. 1502, and gave the particulars of the
cruel deed before his execution. His evidence
is now fully corroborated by the discovery of
the children's bones under the stairs of the
Record-Office in 1664. For Richard's first pang
of conscience regarded the unchristian manner
in which his victims had been buried; and he
ordered the bodies to be lifted and laid in *hal-
lowed ground.* The priest of the Tower found
no spot so secret, and so sacred, as the entrance to his own chapel, in which service was
performed every day. But he died soon after
he had transferred the bodies, and the secret
of the princes' grave was not discovered till
an alteration of the chapel into a depot for
papers revealed it, in the reign of Charles II—
the old chapel being now known as the Record-Office.

MARCIUS,

SON OF CAIUS MARCIUS CORIOLANUS.

PERSONS INTRODUCED.

CAIUS MARCIUS CORIOLANUS.—*A Noble Roman.*
COMINIUS.—*General against the Volscians.*
MENENIUS AGRIPPA.—*Friend to Coriolanus.*
YOUNG MARCIUS.—*Son to Coriolanus.*
AUFIDIUS.—*General of the Volscians.*
VOLUMNIA.—*Mother to Coriolanus.*
VIRGILIA.—*Wife to Coriolanus.*
VALERIA—*Friend to Virgilia.*

MARCIUS,

SON OF CAIUS MARCIUS CORIOLANUS.

"THE Lives of the Noble Grecians and Romans, done into English by Thomas North," is still the best and most robust translation of Plutarch we have; and from this book Shakespeare took the story of Coriolanus; and just as the character was handed down he has copied it.

Coriolanus brings before us the better days of the first military greatness of the Roman people. The monarchy has given way to a republic, but the aristocratic and democratic elements are still at war; and the play is full of the struggle of the two powers—patricians and plebeians, senate and people, consuls and tribunes. In this struggle Coriolanus, in the might of his passions, surpasses even the heroes of the heroic age. But Shakespeare has taken pains to make this exceptional pride and passion possible by giving him a mother glowing with patriotism, and who has centered all her love, pride, and strength in making her only son the chief hero and ruler of his country. She trains him for dangers and ambitions; and is well pleased "to let him seek danger where he was like to find fame."

When Caius Marcius is introduced to us he is in the height and glory of his life. If he can control his passions, he is loved and prized by all; senators stand bare-headed before him, soldiers follow him to battle gladly —he is their god! But, when he is angry, all his good qualities disappear; he disdains his enemies without cause, and they insult him without reason; and the lesson Plutarch extracts from his example is, "that the Muse has imparted nothing finer to mankind than the taming of Nature by moderation and wisdom."

In the opening of the play we see him in one of his extravagantly haughty moods. There has been a severe famine in Rome, to relieve which corn has been sent from Sicily; and Caius Marcius has aroused the populace to fury by a proposition to *sell* instead of to give

it to them. A mutinous crowd of citizens declare him "chief enemy to the people," and
cry—

Let us kill him, and we'll have corn at our own
    price.

  1 CIT. Would you proceed especially against Caius
Marcius?

  2 CIT. Against him first; he's a very dog to the
commonalty.

  1 CIT. Consider you what services he has done
for his country?

  2 CIT. Very well; and could be content to give
him good report for 't, but that he pays himself with
being proud. . . . He did it to please his mother,
and to be partly proud; which he is, even to the
altitude of his virtue. . . . He hath faults, with sur-
plus, to tire in repetition.

Menenius Agrippa, a friend of Caius Marcius, then addresses the people; but his reasoning is interrupted by Caius Marcius himself.
He disdains the populace far too much to give
them good words. If the nobility would only
permit him, he would

                        make a quarry
With thousands of these quarter'd slaves, as high
As I could pick my lance.

His tremendous scorn and passion absolutely silence the mob, and, when he bids them

Go, get you home, you fragments!

they have no answer.

The scene is terminated by the entrance of a messenger bringing word that Rome's enemies, the Volsces, are in arms; and Marcius adds:

The Volsces have much corn; take these rats thither,
To gnaw their garners;

and the citizens steal away. For himself, Marcius is full of joy. The Volsces have a leader called Aufidius, whose nobility and valor even Marcius can envy. If he were not Marcius, he could wish to be Aufidius, for Aufidius is "a lion that he is proud to hunt."

The third scene introduces us to the home of the great soldier. The Roman houses at this time were very simple—a number of rooms all opening into a court. This court, or *atrium*, was the sanctuary of the dwelling, the place of the hearth and the domestic deities; in short, the home-room of the family. For these reasons it was, even at this early date, roofed

over. Benches, chairs, and couches stood in
it; simple seats, low, and without backs, not
unfrequently made of bronze, with rude orna-
mental designs.

In such a room we first see the mother and
wife of Caius Marcius. They are sitting sewing, and talking about the war with the Volces,
and the absence and danger of the beloved son
and husband. The haughty, daring temper of
the mother, Volumnia, is finely contrasted with
the modest sweetness and tender solicitude of
the wife, Virgilia. Volumnia begs her daughter-
in-law to sing, and make herself more comfort-
able in the absence of her husband. For
herself, she says:

When yet he was but tender-bodied, I was pleased
to let him seek danger where he was like to find
fame. To a cruel war I sent him, from whence he
returned, his brows bound with oak.*

VIR. But had he died in the business, madam?
how then?

VOL. Then his good report should have been my
son; I therein would have found issue. Hear me
profess sincerely: Had I a dozen sons, each in my

---

* A garland of oak-leaves was the reward of those who
saved the life of a Roman citizen.

love alike, and none less dear than thine and my
good Marcius, I had rather had eleven die nobly
for their country, than one voluptuously surfeit out
of action.

At this point in their discourse they are
apprised that a Roman lady called Valeria,
who is a friend of Virgilia's, has come to visit
them. This lady is afterward described as—

>   The noble sister of Publicola,
> The moon of Rome; chaste as the icicle,
> That's curded by the frost from purest snow,
> And hangs on Dian's temple.

But Virgilia, full of anxious thoughts, is not
inclined to see her, and wishes to retire. "Indeed, you shall not," answers Volumnia, who
can expect from her son nothing but victory.
"Methinks," she cries—

> Methinks, I hear hither your husband's drum;
> See him pluck Aufidius down by the hair;
> As children from a bear, the Volsces shunning him:
> Methinks, I see him stamp thus, and call thus,—
> *Come on, you cowards, you were got in fear,*
> *Though you were born in Rome :* His bloody brow
> With his mail'd hand then wiping, forth he goes;

Like to a harvest-man, that's task'd to mow
Or all, or lose his hire.

VIR. His bloody brow! O, Jupiter, no blood!

VOL. Away, you fool! it more becomes a man
Than gilt his trophy:—Tell Valeria
We are fit to bid her welcome.

VIR. Heavens bless my lord from fell Aufidius!

VOL. He'll beat Aufidius' head below his knee,
And tread upon his neck.

Enter VALERIA.

VAL. My ladies both, good day to you.

VOL. Sweet madam—

VIR. I am glad to see your ladyship.

VAL. How do you both? you are manifest house-
keepers? What are you sewing here? A fine spot,
in good faith.—How does your little son?

VIR. I thank your ladyship; well, good madam.

VOL. He had rather see the swords, and hear a
drum, than look upon his schoolmaster.

VAL. O' my word, the father's son: I'll swear,
'tis a very pretty boy. O' my troth, I looked upon
him o' Wednesday half an hour together; he has
such a confirmed countenance. I saw him run after
a gilded butterfly, and when he caught it, he let it
go again; and after it again; and over and over he
comes, and up again; catched it again: or whether

his fall enraged him, or how 'twas, he did so set
his teeth, and tear it; O, I warrant, how he mammocked it!

VOL. One of his father's moods.

VAL. Indeed la, 'tis a noble child.

Shakespeare has thrown over this little scene
the very spirit of antiquity. Valeria, like a
courtly lady, knows that nothing can better
please the mother and grandmother than to
talk about and praise the young Marcius; and
an admirable picture she draws of the boy,
who would "rather see the swords and hear a
drum than look upon his schoolmaster." And
could any two words convey better the idea of
a self-willed child than Valeria's description
of his appearance—"he has such a *confirmed
countenance?*" The boyish passion in which he
"mammocked" the gilded butterfly is but the
mimic of the father, "fluttering the Volscians
about, like an eagle in a dove-cote"—while the
grandmother can think of no higher compli-
ment than to proudly pronounce the child to
have been in "one of his father's moods."

In this war with the Volsces, Caius Marcius
performs prodigies of valor; but the proud
conqueror rejects all gifts and rewards.

> I have some wounds upon me, and they smart
> To hear themselves remember'd,

he says. The only favor he desires is the freedom of a poor man who has been kind to him.

> I sometime lay, here in Corioli,
> At a poor man's house; he used me kindly:
> .   .   .   .   . I request you
> To give my poor host freedom.

It is, moreover, agreed, that from this time
for ever—"for what he did before Corioli"—
he shall be called, "with all the applause and
clamor of the host," Caius Marcius Coriolanus
—and by the name of Coriolanus, Caius Marcius is henceforward known.

In the Second Act (Scene III) he is induced
to stand for the consulate; but as soon as he
comes in contact with the people for their suf-
frages he betrays his contempt for them, and
their opinions. They have justice enough to
elect him for his services; but his scorn and
insolence are so apparent that the Tribunes
and he come to bitter words, and one of them
calls him "traitor." From that moment, like a
lion, he lashes himself into a fury, and in the

excitement that follows is condemned to be
thrown from the Tarpeian Rock. However, he
is permitted another hearing, and it is at this
time he utters that grand patriotic prayer—

> The honor'd gods
> Keep Rome in safety, and the chairs of justice
> Supplied with worthy men! plant love among us!
> Throng our large temples with the shows of peace,
> And not our streets with war!

But to the populace he is as haughty as ever;
he "will not buy their mercy at the price of
one fair word;" and he is sentenced to perpetual exile—"never more to enter Rome's
gates." His last words are a defiance. "I
banish you," he cries—

> despising,
> For you, the city, thus I turn my back:
> There is a world elsewhere.

Then Coriolanus offers his services to the
Volsces, and at the head of their armies devas-
tates the Roman territory, until Rome itself is
at his mercy. His revenge seems to be as
strong as his pride. The petitions of his friend
Cominius, who urges their "old acquaintance,

and the drops that they had bled together,'
he absolutely refuses. He will be nameless
"till he has forg'd himself a name i' the fire of
burning Rome." Menenius, "whom he called
father," is ordered "away." Wife, mother,
child, he will not know; "his affairs are ser-
vanted to others"; and any fresh embassies
and suits he will lend no ear unto.

But, as he tells himself that he is firm in
this resolution, his wife and mother approach,
his mother leading the young Marcius by the
hand. Then he feels that he is "not of stronger earth than others." His wife's "doves'
eyes, which can make gods forsworn," plead
with him. His mother bows,

As if Olympus to a molehill should
In supplication nod:

His young boy

Hath an aspect of intercession, which
Great nature cries, *Deny not.*

It is so easy to imagine this child, with his
bold, "confirmed countenance," holding the
hand of his majestic grandmother, dressed in
the white gown bordered with purple, and the

6

golden ball or boss, which Roman boys wore,
hanging from his round, bare throat, mingling
that "aspect of intercession" with a curious,
eager, daring look, that makes the proud, unhappy father pray—

> The god of soldiers,
> With the consent of supreme Jove, inform
> Thy thoughts with nobleness, and stick i' the wars
> Like a great sea-mark, standing every flaw,
> And saving those that eye thee!
>
> .   .   .   .   .   .
>
> That's my brave boy!

Then Volumnia, in a speech of sublime eloquence, pleads for the safety of Rome, and
wins from her angry son the peace which all
the swords of Italy could not have purchased.
It is nearly word for word from Plutarch, with
the charm of meter superadded. Its last argument is-

> This boy that cannot tell what he would have,
> But kneels, and holds up hands, for fellowship,
> Does reason our petition with more strength
> Than thou hast to deny 't.

Yet this boy had shown during the argument, in one quick little speech of defiance,

how perfect a mimic of his uncontrollable
father he was; for, when his grandmother
and mother vow that only over their bodies
shall Coriolanus march to assault his native
city, the child says—

> A shall not tread on me;
> I'll run away till I am bigger, but then I'll fight.

And Coriolanus yields, though conscious that
such yielding is mortal to him.

> O my mother, mother! O!
> You have won a happy victory to Rome:
> But, for your son,—believe it, O, believe it,
> Most dangerously you have with him prevail'd,
> If not most mortal to him.

His prophecy is rapidly verified. His old
rival and enemy, Aufidius, accuses him before
the lords of Antium of having given up—

> For certain drops of salt your city of Rome
> (I say your city) to his wife and mother.

In the contention that follows, Coriolanus breaks
out into one of his passionate rages, and dies
under the swords of the Volscian lords.

An American poet—Walt Whitman—says

that Coriolanus is incarnated, uncompromising feudalism in literature (" Democratic Vistas," p. 81). But Coriolanus is not altogether a political play; for, though it is the history of a struggle between patricians and plebeians, it is also the history of a struggle between Coriolanus and his own self. And it is not the Roman people who bring about his destruction; it is his own haughty pride and passionate self-will. The lesson that Shakespeare teaches us in Coriolanus is the lesson Plutarch found there—"the Muse has imparted nothing finer to mankind than the taming of Nature by moderation and wisdom."

HISTORICAL SKETCH

OF

CORIOLANUS.

THE story of Coriolanus must be founded upon legend or tradition; for its date is given at the 260th, or, according to some, at the 290th year of Rome, at least 500 years before Plutarch wrote. Livy, the Roman historian, wrote the story a century earlier; but in no essential point does it differ from that of Plutarch. It must be noted, also, that some historians say that Coriolanus, though he joined the enemies of Rome, died honored and beloved among them; and that even among his own people his memory was reverenced.

Shakespeare did not probably know this version; if he had, he would not have adopted it; for he had to show that the false step Coriolanus took, and his proud resentment, hurried him upon a course which brought evils worse than the Tarpeian Rock.

PERSONS IN THE DRAMA.

CYMBELINE.—*King of Britain.*

CLOTEN.—*Son to the Queen by a former Husband.*

LEONATUS POSTHUMUS.—*Husband to Imogen.*

BELARIUS.—*A Banished Lord, disguised under the name of Morgan.*

GUIDERIUS. } *Sons to Cymbeline, disguised under the names of*
ARVIRAGUS. }   *Polydore and Cadwal, supposed sons of Belarius.*

LUCIUS.—*General of the Roman Forces.*

PISANIO.—*Servant to Posthumus.*

QUEEN.—*Wife to Cymbeline.*

IMOGEN.—*Daughter to Cymbeline by a former Queen.*

GUIDERIUS AND ARVIRAGUS,

SONS OF CYMBELINE, KING OF BRITAIN.

GUIDERIUS AND ARVIRAGUS,

SONS OF CYMBELINE, KING OF BRITAIN.

THE "marvelous drama" of Cymbeline belongs to the heathen times of the aboriginal
Britons; but to that bright period of it when
Roman civilization had exerted over the people a wide and beneficent influence. In it
Leonatus is made to boast at Rome of his
"accomplished countrymen" as—

Men more order'd, than when Julius Cæsar
Smil'd at their lack of skill, but found their courage
Worthy his frowning at: Their discipline
(Now mingled with their courages) will make known
To their opposers, they are people such
That mend upon the world.

. Holinshed afforded Shakespeare materials
for the first part of the play—namely, the dispute about the tribute-money, and the war be-

tween Britain and Rome. He tells us that
Cymbeline began to reign in the nineteenth
year of the Emperor Augustus, and that both
Cymbeline and his sons Guiderius and Arviragus are mentioned as historical characters.
Cymbeline was one of the most powerful and
wealthy of the ancient British kings. His capital was Camalodunum, now either Maldon or
Colchester. It was the first Roman colony in
Britain, and a place of great magnificence ;
therefore the supposition of luxury in dress
and in household arrangements is not unnatural in the play. Roman luxury speedily followed Roman colonization ; and, besides, Cymbeline and his ancestors were constantly in
commercial intercourse with the Greeks and
Phœnicians.

It is very likely that Cymbeline's palace
had all the characteristics of a Roman villa,
and therefore the play opens in "the garden
behind Cymbeline's palace" without violating
any probability. In this garden two gentlemen of the court are discussing the marriage
of Imogen, the daughter of Cymbeline, with
Leonatus, a noble youth, reared under the
special care and protection of the King, who

had given him "all the learnings that his time
could make him the receiver of"; and who
lived at the court, "most prais'd, most lov'd;
a sample to the youngest."

But this marriage had been clandestine, and
had greatly angered Cymbeline; for Imogen
was the heiress of his throne, and he wished
to unite her with Cloten, the son of his queen
by a former marriage; a braggart inheriting
from his mother the basest and most degrad-
ing vices; "a thing too bad for bad report";
while Leonatus is

> a creature such
> As to seek through the regions of the earth
> For one his like, there would be something failing
> In him that should compare.
>
> 2 GENT.   I honor him
> Even out of your report. But, pray you, tell me,
> Is she sole child to the king?
>
> 1 GENT.   His only child.
> He had two sons (if this be worth your hearing,
> Mark it), the eldest of them at three years old,
> I' the swathing clothes the other, from their nursery
> Were stolen; and to this hour no guess in knowledge
> Which way they went.
>
>   2 GENT. That a king's children should be so con-
>   vey'd,

So slackly guarded! and the search so slow,
That could not trace them!

   1 GENT.   Howsoe'er 'tis strange,
Or that the negligence may well be laughed at,
Yet is it true, sir.

   2 GENT.   I do well believe you.

These two princes had really been stolen
by a faithful and famous warrior of Cymbeline's court, called Belarius, who, by valuable
services, had well deserved the favor of his
king.   But suddenly Cymbeline's anger fell
upon the guiltless hero.   Two villains swore
falsely that he had made a treacherous league
with the Romans, and Cymbeline deprived him
of his possessions and banished him.

The old soldier, unable to get justice, determined, at least, to have revenge.   He carried off the two sons of Cymbeline with the
help of their nurse; her he married, and he
brought up the boys as his own children, in a
solitary cavern in the mountains of Wales.   In
this seclusion he trained them to hunting and
all manly exercises, and they grew up true,
simple, brave, inspired with a mixed spirit
of strength and gentleness, of modesty and

Hail, Heaven!

Guiderius and Arviragus.

ambition, the "sweetest companions in the world."

We are first introduced to the youths in the Third Scene of the Third Act, than which there are few finer things in Shakespeare. The breath of the old innocent world is over it, the thoughts and feelings of generous youth, and the wisdom of a good old age.

SCENE III.—Wales. *A Mountainous Country, with a Cave.*

Enter BELARIUS, GUIDERIUS, *and* ARVIRAGUS.

BEL. A goodly day not to keep house, with such
Whose roof's as low as ours. Stoop, boys: this gate
Instructs you how t' adore the heavens, and bows you
To a morning's holy office: the gates of monarchs
Are arch'd so high that giants may get through
And keep their impious turbans on, without
Good morrow to the sun.—Hail, thou fair heaven!
We house i' the rock, yet use thee not so hardly
As prouder livers do.

GUI.   Hail, heaven!

ARV.   Hail, heaven!

BEL. Now, for our mountain sport. Up to yon hill:
Your legs are young; I'll tread these flats. Consider,
When you above perceive me like a crow,

That it is place which lessens and sets off;
And you may then revolve what tales I have told you,
Of courts, of princes, of the tricks in war;
This service is not service, so being done,
But being so allow'd; to apprehend thus,
Draws us a profit from all things we see;
And often, to our comfort, shall we find
The sharded beetle in a safer hold
Than is the full-wing'd eagle. O! this life
Is nobler, than attending for a check;
Richer, than doing nothing for a bribe;
Prouder, than rustling in unpaid-for silk:
Such gain the cap of him that makes him fine,
Yet keeps his book uncross'd.* No life to ours.

   Gui. Out of your proof you speak: we, poor un-
       fledg'd,
Have never wing'd from view o' the nest; nor know not
What air 's from home. Haply, this life is best,
If quiet life be best; sweeter to you,
That have a sharper known; well corresponding
With your stiff age; but unto us it is
A cell of ignorance, traveling abed,
A prison for a debtor, that not dares
To stride a limit.

---

   * "Yet keeps his book uncross'd." The tradesman's book
was *crossed* when the account was paid. In old writers the
allusion to this circumstance is frequent.

ARV.   What should we speak of,
When we are old as you? when we shall hear
The rain and wind beat dark December, how
In this our pinching cave shall we discourse
The freezing hours away? We have seen nothing:
We are beastly: subtle as the fox for prey;
Like warlike as the wolf for what we eat:
Our valor is, to chase what flies; our cage
We make a quire, as doth the prison'd bird,
And sing our bondage freely.

BEL.   How you speak
Did you but know the city's usuries,
And felt them knowingly: the art o' the court,
As hard to leave, as keep; whose top to climb
Is certain falling, or so slippery that
The fear 's as bad as falling: the toil of the war,
A pain that only seems to seek out danger
I' the name of fame and honor; which dies i' the
     search,
And hath as oft a slanderous epitaph,
As record of fair act; nay, many times,
Doth ill deserve by doing well; what's worse,
Must court'sy at the censure.—O, boys! this story
The world may read in me: my body's mark'd
With Roman swords, and my report was once
First with the best of note. Cymbeline lov'd me;
And when a soldier was the theme, my name

Was not far off: then was I as a tree,
Whose boughs did bend with fruit; but, in one night,
A storm, or robbery, call it what you will,
Shook down my mellow hangings, nay, my leaves,
And left me bare to weather.
    Gui.   Uncertain favor!
    Bel. My fault being nothing (as I have told you
      oft)
But that two villains, whose false oaths prevail'd
Before my perfect honor, swore to Cymbeline
I was confederate with the Romans: so,
Follow'd my banishment;

    .   .   .   .

                 But, up to the mountains;
This is not hunter's language.—He that strikes
The venison first shall be lord o' the feast;
To him the other two shall minister,
And we will fear no poison, which attends
In place of greater state.   I'll meet you in the valleys.
                   [*Exeunt* Gui. *and* Arv.
How hard it is to hide the sparks of nature!
These boys know little they are sons to the king;
Nor Cymbeline dreams that they are alive.
They think they are mine; and, though train'd up
      thus meanly
I' the cave wherein they bow, their thoughts do hit
The roofs of palaces; and nature prompts them,

In simple and low things, to prince it, much
Beyond the trick of others. This Polydore,—
The heir of Cymbeline and Britain, whom
The king, his father, called Guiderius,—Jove!
When on my three-foot stool I sit, and tell
The warlike feats I have done, his spirits fly out
Into my story: say,—"Thus mine enemy fell;
And thus I set my foot on 's neck;" even then
The princely blood flows in his cheek, he sweats,
Strains his young nerves, and puts himself in posture
That acts my words. The younger brother, Cadwal
(Once Arviragus) in as like a figure,
Strikes life into my speech, and shows much more
His own conceiving. Hark! the game is rous'd!—
O Cymbeline! heaven, and my conscience, knows
Thou didst unjustly banish me; whereon
At three, and two years old, I stole these babes,
Thinking to bar thee of succession, as
Thou reft'st me of my lands. Euriphile,
Thou wast their nurse; they took thee for their
      mother,
And every day do honor to her grave:
Myself, Belarius, that am Morgan call'd,
They take for natural father.—The game is up.

                              [*Exit.*

At this very hour Imogen, the unknown
sister of the two boys, is approaching their

cave, in the disguise of a page. She has been
driven to this course by the persecution following her contempt for the Queen's son, Cloten, and her love for her husband, Leonatus.
There is nothing in this love but what is beautiful and worthy of honor. They have grown
up together; it is a love of all their life-time
that unites them. Their marriage in the temple
of Jupiter was an act of self-defense against the
cruel, selfish ambition of Imogen's stepmother;
but the King, her father, being thoroughly under the influence of his wicked queen, banishes
Leonatus, and confines Imogen.

Imogen is one of the most lovely and art-
less characters which Shakespeare imagined.
Her appearance sheds warmth, fragrance, and
brightness over the whole drama. She yields
to her father's anger with filial duty, but she
is ever faithful to her husband. In her parting sorrow she forgets what she had intended
to say. She would have told him at what
time she "was in heaven" praying for him; at
what hours he "could encounter her with ori-
sons." When he is away she thinks only of
him. She wears his letters next her heart.
Before she opens them, she prays with touch-

ing gladness for "good news." Going to bed
at midnight, she thinks of him, and kisses his
bracelet, and at night she weeps when she remembers him "'twixt clock and clock." Neither
the anger of her father, the falseness of her stepmother, nor the insolence of the rude Cloten,
makes her complain ; she is patient, joyous, in-
genuous, bears no resentment for injuries ; nor
do suffering and trouble press too heavily on
her.

At length her position at her father's court
becomes intolerable ; Pisanio, her servant, advises her to seek her husband in Rome, and
for this end to enter the service of Lucius,
the Roman general in Britain, in the service of
a page. "Lucius, the Roman, comes to Milford-Haven to-morrow," he urges her, and—

> Now, if you could wear a mind
> Dark as your fortune is, and but disguise
> That which, t' appear itself, must not yet be
> But by self-danger, you should tread a course
> Pretty, and full of view : yea, haply, near
> The residence of Posthumus.
>
> .   .   .   .   .   .
>
> Forethinking this, I have already fit
> ('Tis in my cloak-bag) doublet, hat, hose, all

That answer to them :   .   .   .
.   .   .   'fore noble Lucius
Present yourself, desire his service.   .   .   .
.   .   .   .   .   he's honorable,
And, doubling that, most holy.
   IMO.   Thou art all the comfort
The gods will diet me with.   Pr'ithee, away :
There's more to be considered ; but we'll even
All that good time will give us.

In this disguise of a page, Imogen is especially charming, because she is quite unable to
lay aside her sweet feminine nature.   In addi-
tion, this friend gives her a box, which he received from the Queen, and which he assures
her, if she be sick, contains a medicine to
" drive away distemper."

SCENE VI.—*Before the Cave of* Belarius.   Enter
   IMOGEN *in Boy's Clothes.*

   IMO. I see, a man's life is a tedious one;
I have tir'd myself, and for two nights together
Have made the ground my bed.   I should be sick,
But that my resolution helps me.—Milford,
When from the mountain-top Pisanio show'd thee,
Thou wast within a ken.   O Jove! I think

Foundations fly the wretched; such, I mean,
Where they should be reliev'd.   Two beggars told me
I could not miss my way: will poor folks lie,
That have afflictions on them, knowing 'tis
A punishment or trial?   Yes; no wonder,
When rich ones scarce tell true: to lapse in fullness
Is sorer than to lie for need; and falsehood
Is worse in kings than beggars.—My dear lord!
.   .   .   .   Now I think on thee,
My hunger's gone; but even before, I was
At point to sink for food.—But what is this?
Here is a path to it: 'tis some savage hold:
I were best not call; I dare not call; yet famine,
Ere clean it o'erthrow nature, makes it valiant.
Plenty, and peace, breeds cowards; hardness ever
Of hardness is mother.—Ho!   Who's here?
If anything that's civil, speak; if savage,
Take, or lend.—Ho!—No answer? then I'll enter.
Best draw my sword; and if mine enemy
But fear the sword like me, he'll scarcely look on't.
Such a foe, good heavens!

Enter BELARIUS, GUIDERIUS, *and* ARVIRAGUS.

BEL. You, Polydore, have prov'd best woodman, and
Are master of the feast: Cadwal, and I,
Will play the cook and servant; 'tis our match:

The sweat of industry would dry, and die,
But for the end it works to.   Come; our stomachs
Will make what's homely, savory: Weariness
Can snore upon the flint, when rusty sloth
Finds the down pillow hard.—Now, peace be here,
Poor house, that keep'st thyself!

Gui.   I am thoroughly weary.

Arv. I am weak with toil, yet strong in appetite.

Gui. There is cold meat i' the cave: we'll browse
    on that
Whilst what we have kill'd be cook'd.

Bel.   Stay: come not in.
                                      [*Looking in.*

But that it eats our victuals, I should think
Here were a fairy.

Gui.   What's the matter, sir?

Bel. By Jupiter, an angel! or, if not,
An earthly paragon!—Behold divineness
No elder than a boy!

Enter Imogen.

Imo. Good masters, harm me not:
Before I enter'd here, I call'd; and thought
To have begg'd, or bought, what I have took.   Good
    troth,
I have stolen nought; nor would not, though I had
    found
Gold strew'd o' the floor.   Here's money for my meat:

Guiderius, Arviragus, and Imogen.

Guiderius and Arviragus.

I would have left it on the board, so soon
As I had made my meal, and parted
With prayers for the provider.

GUI.   Money, youth?

ARV. All gold and silver rather turn to dirt!
As 'tis no better reckoned, but of those
Who worship dirty gods.

IMO.   I see, you are angry.
Know, if you kill me for my fault, I should
Have died, had I not made it.

BEL.   Whither bound?

IMO. To Milford-Haven.

BEL.   What's your name?

IMO. Fidele, sir. I have a kinsman who
Is bound for Italy: he embark'd at Milford;
To whom being going, almost spent with hunger,
I am fallen in this offence.

BEL.   Prithee, fair youth,
Think us no churls, nor measure our good minds
By this rude place we live in. Well encounter'd.
'Tis almost night: you shall have better cheer
Ere you depart; and thanks, to stay and eat it.—
Boys, bid him welcome.

GUI.   Were you a woman, youth,
I should woo hard but be your groom.—In honesty,
I bid for you as I do buy.

ARV.   I'll make 't my comfort,

He is a man: I'll love him as my brother;
And such a welcome as I'd give to him,
After long absence, such is yours.—Most welcome.
Be sprightly, for you fall 'mongst friends.

IMO.   'Mongst friends!
If brothers? [*Aside.*] Would it had been so, that they
Had been my father's sons: then, had my prize
Been less; and so more equal ballasting
To thee, Posthumus.

BEL.   He wrings at some distress.

GUI. Would I could free 't!

ARV.   Or I; whate'er it be,
What pain it cost, what danger. Gods!

BEL.   Hark, boys! [*Whispering.*

IMO. Great men,
That had a court no bigger than this cave,
That did attend themselves, and had the virtue
Which their own conscience seal'd them (laying by
That nothing gift of differing multitudes),
Could not out-peer these twain. Pardon me, gods!
I'd change my sex to be companion with them,
Since Leonatus false.

BEL.   It shall be so.
Boys, we'll go dress our hunt.—Fair youth, come in:
Discourse is heavy, fasting; when we have supp'd,
We'll mannerly demand thee of thy story,
So far as thou wilt speak it.

Gui.   Pray, draw near.

Arv. The night to the owl, and morn to the lark,
 less welcome.

Imo. Thanks, sir.

Arv.   I pray, draw near.

The First Scene in the Fourth Act shows
us that Imogen's flight has been closely followed by her rude suitor, Cloten, the Queen's
son. He appears near the cave of Belarius,
and in his soliloquy tells himself that within
an hour he will "spurn her home to her
father, who may haply be a little angry for
my so rough usage, but my mother, having
power over his testiness, shall turn all into my
commendations."

But Imogen is in the cave with her friends;
sick and weary with sorrow and fatigue, and
only waiting their departure to the hunt, in
order to take the medicine given to her by
Pisanio, when he furnished her with her disguise at their parting. This medicine, given
him by the Queen, he supposed to be a sovereign remedy in all sickness; and the Queen
supposed it to be a poison, for she hated
Pisanio, knowing him to be true to Imogen
and Leonatus. However, she also was de-

7

ceived, for the physician from whom she obtained it, suspecting her of evil intentions,
had substituted for poison a powerful narcotic,
which would induce a death-like trance, but in
no way injure life.

Before the Cave.

BELARIUS, GUIDERIUS, ARVIRAGUS, *and* IMOGEN.

BEL. You are not well [*To* IMOGEN]: remain here
    in the cave;
We'll come to you after hunting.

ARV.   Brother, stay here:
[*To* IMOGEN.   Are we not brothers?

IMO.   So man and man should be;
But clay and clay differs in dignity,
Whose dust is both alike.   I am very sick.

GUI. Go you to hunting; I'll abide with him.

IMO. So sick I am not,—yet I am not well;
But not so citizen a wanton, as
To seem to die, ere sick.   So please you, leave
    me;
Stick to your journal course: the breach of cus-
    tom
Is breach of all.   I am ill; but your being by me
Can not amend me: society is no comfort
To one not sociable.   I am not very sick,
Since I can reason of it: pray you, trust me here;

I'll rob none but myself, and let me die,
Stealing so poorly.

GUI.   I love thee; I have spoke it:
How much the quantity, the weight as much,
As I do love my father.

BEL.   What! how? how?

ARV. If it be sin to say so, sir, I yoke me
In my good brother's fault: I know not why
I love this youth; and I have heard you say,
Love's reason's without reason: . . .

 . . . . Brother, farewell.

IMO. I wish ye sport.

ARV.   You health.—So please you, sir.

IMO. [*Aside.*] These are kind creatures. Gods,
  what lies I have heard!
Our courtiers say, all's savage but at court:
Experience, O! thou disprov'st report.

 . . . .

I am sick still; heart-sick.—Pisanio,
I'll now taste of thy drug.

GUI.   I could not stir him:
He said he was gentle, but unfortunate;
Dishonestly afflicted, but yet honest.

ARV. Thus did he answer me; yet said, hereafter
I might know more.

BEL.   To the field, to the field!—
We'll leave you for this time; go in, and rest.

Arv. We'll not be long away.

Bel.   Pray, be not sick
For you must be our housewife.

Imo.   Well, or ill,
I am bound to you.

Bel.   And shalt be ever. [*Exit* Imogen.
This youth, howe'er distress'd he appears, hath had
Good ancestors.

Arv.   How angel-like he sings!

Gui. But his neat cookery: he cut our roots in
        characters;
And sauc'd our broths, as Juno had been sick,
And he her dieter.

Arv.   Nobly he yokes
A smiling with a sigh, as if the sigh
Was that it was, for not being such a smile;
The smile mocking the sigh, that it would fly
From so divine a temple, to commix
With winds that sailors rail at.

Gui.   I do note
That grief and patience, rooted in him both,
Mingle their spurs together.

Arv.   Grow, patience!
And let the stinking elder, grief, untwine
His perishing root with the increasing vine!

Bel. It is great morning. Come; away!—Who's
        there?

Enter CLOTEN.

CLO. I can not find those runagates. . . .

BEL.   Those runagates!
Means he not us? I partly know him; 'tis
Cloten, the son o' the queen. I fear some am-
    bush.
I saw him not these many years, and yet
I know 'tis he.—We are held as outlaws:—hence.

GUI. He is but one. You and my brother
    search
What companies are near: pray you, away;
Let me alone with him.   [*Exeunt* BEL. *and* ARV.

CLO.   Soft! What are you
That fly me thus? some villain mountaineers?
I have heard of such.—What slave art thou?

GUI.   A thing
More slavish did I ne'er, than answering
A slave without a knock.

CLO.   Thou art a robber,
A law-breaker, a villain. Yield thee, thief.

GUI. To whom? to thee? What art thou? Have
    not I
An arm as big as thine? a heart as big?
Thy words, I grant, are bigger; for I wear not
My dagger in my mouth. Say, what thou art,
Why I should yield to thee?

CLO.   Thou villain base,

Know'st me not by my clothes?

GUI.   No, nor thy tailor, rascal,
Who is thy grandfather? he made those clothes,
Which, as it seems, make thee.

CLO.   Thou precious varlet,
My tailor made them not.

GUI.   Hence, then, and thank
The man that gave them thee. Thou art some
        fool;
I am loath to beat thee.

CLO.   Thou injurious thief,
Hear but my name, and tremble.

GUI.   What's thy name?

CLO. Cloten, thou villain.

GUI. Cloten, thou double villain, be thy name,
I can not tremble at it: were 't toad, or adder,
        spider,
'Twould move me sooner.

CLO.   To thy farther fear,
Nay, to thy mere confusion, thou shalt know
I'm son to the queen.

GUI.   I am sorry for 't; not seeming
So worthy as thy birth.

CLO.   Art not afeard?

GUI. Those that I reverence, those I fear, the
        wise:
At fools I laugh, not fear them.

Clo.   Die the death.
When I have slain thee with my proper hand,
I'll follow those that even now fled hence,
And on the gates of Lud's town set your heads.
Yield, rustic mountaineer.   [*Exeunt, fighting.*

Enter Belarius *and* Arviragus.

Bel. No company's abroad.
Arv. None in the world. You did mistake him,
    sure.
Bel. I can not tell: long is it since I saw him,
But time hath nothing blurr'd those lines of favor
Which then he wore: the snatches in his voice,
And burst of speaking, were as his. I am absolute
'Twas very Cloten.
Arv.   In this place we left them:
I wish my brother make good time with him,
You say he is so fell.
Bel.   Being scarce made up,
I mean, to man, he had not apprehension
Of roaring terrors; for th' effect of judgment
Is oft the cause of fear. But see, thy brother.

Re-enter Guiderius *with* Cloten's *head.*

Gui. This Cloten was a fool, an empty purse,—
There was no money in 't. Not Hercules

Could have knock'd out his brains, for he had
    none;
Yet I not doing this, the fool had borne
My head, as I do his.

    Bel.   What hast thou done?
    Gui. I am perfect what:* cut off one Cloten's
    head,
Son to the queen, after his own report;
Who call'd me traitor, mountaineer; and swore,
With his own single hand he'd take us in,
Displace our heads, where (thank the gods!) they
    grow,
And set them on Lud's town.

    Bel.   We are all undone.
    Gui. Why, worthy father, what have we to lose,
But, that he swore to take, our lives? The law
Protects not us; then, why should we be tender,
To let an arrogant piece of flesh threat us,
Play judge, and executioner, all himself,
For we do fear the law? What company
Discover you abroad?

    Bel.   No single soul
Can we set eye on, but in all safe reason
He must have some attendants. Though his humor
Was nothing but mutation—ay, and that
From one bad thing to worse; not frenzy, not

---

    * That is, I am perfectly aware what I have done.

Absolute madness, could so far have rav'd,
To bring him here alone.

  .   .   .   .   .   .

ARV.   Let ordinance
Come as the gods foresay it: howsoe'er,
My brother hath done well.

BEL.   I had no mind
To hunt this day: the boy Fidele's sickness
Did make my way long forth.

GUI.   With his own sword,
Which he did wave against my throat, I have ta'en
His head from him: I'll throw 't into the creek
Behind our rock; and let it to the sea,
And tell the fishes he's the queen's son, Cloten:
That's all I reck.   [*Exit.*

BEL.   I fear 'twill be reveng'd.
Would, Polydore, thou hadst not done 't, though valor
Becomes thee well enough.

ARV.   Would I had done 't,
So the revenge alone pursued me!—Polydore,
I love thee brotherly, but envy much
Thou hast robb'd me of this deed: I would, revenges,
That possible strength might meet, would seek us
    through,
And put us to our answer.

BEL.   Well, 'tis done.
We'll hunt no more to-day, nor seek for danger

Where there's no profit. I prithee, to our rock:
You and Fidele play the cooks; I'll stay
Till hasty Polydore return, and bring him
To dinner presently.

    ARV.   Poor sick Fidele!
I'll willingly to him: to gain his color,
I'd let a parish of such Clotens blood,
And praise myself for charity.   [*Exit.*

    BEL.   O thou goddess,
Thou divine Nature, how thyself thou blazon'st
In these two princely boys! They are as gentle
As zephyrs blowing below the violet,
Not wagging his sweet head; and yet as rough,
Their royal blood enchaf'd, as the rud'st wind,
That by the top doth take the mountain pine,
And make him stoop to the vale. 'Tis wonder
That an invisible instinct should frame them
To royalty unlearn'd, honor untaught,
Civility not seen from other, valor
That wildly grows in them, but yields a crop
As if it had been sow'd! .   .   .

   .   .   .   .

Re-enter GUIDERIUS.

    GUI.   Where's my brother?
I have sent Cloten's clotpoll down the stream,
In embassy to his mother: his body's hostage
For his return.   [*Solemn music.*

BEL. My ingenious instrument!
Hark, Polydore, it sounds; but what occasion
Hath Cadwal now to give it motion? Hark!
GUI. Is he at home?
BEL. He went hence even now.
GUI. What does he mean? since death of my
dear'st mother
It did not speak before. All solemn things
Should answer solemn accidents. The matter?

.   .   .   .   .   .

Re-enter ARVIRAGUS, *bearing* IMOGEN *as dead in his
arms.*

BEL. Look! here he comes,
And brings the dire occasion in his arms,
Of what we blame him for.
ARV. The bird is dead,
That we have made so much on. I had rather
Have skipp'd from sixteen years of age to sixty,
To have turn'd my leaping time into a crutch,
Than have seen this.
GUI. O sweetest, fairest lily!
My brother wears thee not the one half so well,
As when thou grew'st thyself.
BEL. O, melancholy!

.   .   .   .

Jove knows what man thou mightst have made; but I,
Thou diedst, a most rare boy, of melancholy.—

How found you him?

ARV.   Stark, as you see:
Thus smiling, as some fly had tickled slumber,
Not as death's dart, being laugh'd at: his right cheek
Reposing on a cushion.

GUI.   Where?

ARV.   O' the floor;
His arms thus leagued: I thought he slept, and put
My clouted brogues from off my feet, whose rudeness
Answer'd my steps too loud.

GUI.   Why, he but sleeps:
If he be gone, he'll make his grave a bed;
With female fairies will his tomb be haunted,
And worms will not come to thee.

ARV.   With fairest flowers,
Whilst summer lasts, and I live here, Fidele,
I'll sweeten thy sad grave: thou shalt not lack
The flower that's like thy face, pale primrose; nor
The azur'd hare-bell, like thy veins; no, nor
The leaf of eglantine, whom not to slander,
Out-sweeten'd not thy breath: the ruddock* would,
With charitable bill, ...

    .   .   .   .   bring thee all this;
Yea, and furr'd moss besides, when flowers are none,
To winter-ground thy corse.

* The robin red-breast.

Gui.   Prithee, have done;
And do not play in wench-like words with that
Which is so serious.   Let us bury him,
And not protract with admiration what
Is now due debt.—To the grave.

Arv.   Say, where shall 's lay him?

Gui. By good Euriphile, our mother.

Arv.   Be 't so.

.   .   .   .

Gui. Nay, Cadwal, we must lay his head to the
    east;
My father hath a reason for 't.

Arv.   'Tis true.

Gui. Come on then, and remove him.

Arv.   So,—Begin.

SONG.

Gui. *Fear no more the heat o' the sun,*
        Nor the furious winter's rages;
      Thou thy worldly task hast done,
        Home art gone, and ta'en thy wages:
      Golden lads and girls all must,
      As chimney-sweepers, come to dust.

Arv. *Fear no more the frown o' the great,*
        Thou art past the tyrant's stroke;
      Care no more to clothe and eat,
        To thee the reed is as the oak:

> *The scepter, learning, physic, must*
> *All follow this, and come to dust.*

GUI. *Fear no more the lightning-flash,*
ARV.   *Nor th' all-dreaded thunder-stone;*
GUI. *Fear not slander, censure rash;*
ARV.   *Thou hast finish'd joy and moan:*
BOTH. *All lovers young, all lovers must*
  Consign to thee, and come to dust.

GUI. *No exorciser harm thee!*
ARV.   *Nor no witchcraft charm thee!*
GUI. *Ghost unlaid forbear thee!*
ARV.   *Nothing ill come near thee!*
BOTH. *Quiet consummation have;*
  And renowned be thy grave!

GUI. We have done our obsequies. Come, lay
  him down.
BEL. Here's a few flowers, but 'bout midnight
  more:
The herbs that have on them cold dew o' the night
Are strewings fitt'st for graves.—   .   .
  .   .   .   .

Come on, away: apart upon our knees.
  [*Exeunt* BELARIUS, GUIDERIUS, *and* ARVIRAGUS.

But before the midnight could give them
for her burial "herbs that have on them cold

dew o' the night," Imogen awoke, the power
of the sleeping potion being exhausted. Ere
she could determine on anything, Lucius, the
Roman general, with some of his officers, sur-
prised her, and she gladly accepted the position of page to Lucius. For Lucius has been
ordered by the Roman Senate to make war on
Cymbeline, who has refused to pay the tribute
which his uncle Cassibelan agreed with Julius
Cæsar to render to Rome yearly. The legions
from Gallia have crossed the sea and are now
at Milford-Haven, and Imogen hopes that her
banished husband is with them.

The noise of the gathering of soldiers, and
of the preparation for war, is on every side,
and has reached Belarius and his foster-sons in
their cave. Belarius would willingly escape
from the strife, but the two young princes are
eager for the fight.

GUI. The noise is round about us.
BEL.   Let us from it.
ARV. What pleasure, sir, find we in life, to lock it
From action and adventure?
GUI.   Nay, what hope
Have we in hiding us? this way, the Romans
Must or for Britons slay us, or receive us

For barbarous and unnatural revolts
During their use, and slay us after.

BEL.   Sons,
We'll higher to the mountains; there secure us.
To the king's party there's no going: newness
Of Cloten's death (we being not known, not muster'd
Among the bands) may drive us to a render
Where we have liv'd; and so extort from's that
Which we have done, whose answer would be death
Drawn on with torture.

GUI.   This is, sir, a doubt,
In such a time nothing becoming you,
Nor satisfying us.

ARV.   It is not likely
That when they hear the Roman horses neigh,
Behold their quarter'd fires, have both their eyes
And ears so cloy'd importantly as now,
That they will waste their time upon our note,
To know from whence we are.

BEL.   O! I am known
Of many in the army: many years,
Though Cloten then but young, you see, not wore
    him
From my remembrance: and, besides, the king
Hath not deserv'd my service, nor your loves,
Who find in my exile the want of breeding,
The certainty of this hard life; aye, hopeless

To have the courtesy your cradle promis'd,
But to be still hot summer's tanlings, and
The shrinking slaves of winter.

GUI.   Than be so,
Better to cease to be.   Pray, sir, to the army:
I and my brother are not known; yourself,
So out of thought, and thereto so o'ergrown,
Can not be question'd.

ARV.   By this sun that shines,
I'll thither: What thing is 't, that I never
Did see man die? scarce ever look'd on blood,
But that of coward hares, hot goats, and venison?
Never bestrid a horse, save one, that had
A rider like myself, who ne'er wore rowel,
Nor iron, on his heel?   I am asham'd
To look upon the holy sun, to have
The benefit of his bless'd beams, remaining
So long a poor unknown.

GUI.   By heavens, I'll go.
If you will bless me, sir, and give me leave,
I'll take the better care; but if you will not,
The hazard therefore due fall on me by
The hands of Romans.

ARV.   So say I.   Amen.

BEL.   No reason I, since of your lives you set
So slight a valuation, should reserve
My crack'd one to more care.   Have with you, boys.

If in your country wars you chance to die,
That is my bed too, lads, and there I'll lie:
Lead, lead.—[*Aside.*] The time seems long;   their
   blood thinks scorn,
Till it fly out, and show them princes born.

In the battle that ensues, the Britons are
defeated and fly, and Cymbeline is taken prisoner. But in a narrow lane, "close by the
battle, ditch'd, and wall'd with turf," the Romans are held at bay by Belarius, Guiderius,
Arviragus, and Leonatus, who is in the disguise
of a common British soldier. By their desperate valor, the fortune of the day is turned and
Cymbeline rescued. Leonatus himself tells a
Roman lord, after the battle, how "an ancient
soldier with a white beard, and two striplings,
lads more like to run a country game than to
commit such slaughter,"

Made good the passage; cried to those that fled,
"Our Britain's harts die flying, not our men:
To darkness fleet souls that fly backward!   Stand;
   .   .   .   .   . Stand, stand!"

And thus how

"Two boys, an old man twice a boy, a lane,
Preserv'd the Britons, was the Romans' bane."

The Britons themselves regard their triumph as miraculous. One British captain cries out:

Great Jupiter be prais'd! Lucius is taken.
'Tis thought the old man and his sons were angels.

2 CAP. There was a fourth man, in a silly habit,
That gave th' affront with them.

1 CAP.   So 'tis reported;
But none of them can be found.

Scene V opens in Cymbeline's tent soon after the victory, and Belarius and the two unknown princes are with the king.   ·

CYM. Stand by my side, you whom the gods have
    made
Preservers of my throne. Woe is my heart,
That the poor soldier, that so richly fought,
Whose rags sham'd gilded arms, whose naked breast
Stepp'd before targes of proof, can not be found:
He shall be happy that can find him, if
Our grace can make him so.

BEL.   I never saw
Such noble fury in so poor a thing;
Such precious deeds in one that promis'd naught
But beggary and poor looks.

·   ·   ·   ·   ·   ·   ·

CYM.   'Tis now the time
To ask of whence you are:—report it.

BEL.   Sir,
In Cambria are we born, and gentlemen.
Further to boast, were neither true nor modest,
Unless I add, we are honest.
    CYM.   Bow your knees.
Arise, my knights o' the battle: I create you
Companions to our person, and will fit you
With dignities becoming your estates.

Then Lucius, the Roman general, attended
by Imogen as his page, is led into Cymbeline's
presence as a prisoner. For himself it sufficeth
that "a Roman with a Roman's heart can
suffer"; but for Imogen he entreats mercy.

        .   .   .   . my boy, a Briton born,
Let him be ransom'd: never master had
A page so kind, so duteous, diligent,
So tender over his occasions, true,
So feat, so nurse-like. Let his virtue join
With my request, which, I'll make bold, your high-
        ness
Can not deny: he hath done no Briton harm,
Though he have serv'd a Roman. Save him, sir,
And spare no blood beside.
    CYM.   I have surely seen him:
His favor is familiar to me.—Boy,

Thou hast look'd thyself into my grace,
And art mine own.

    .   .   .   .

IMO.   I humbly thank your highness.

    .   .   .   .

CYM.   What's thy name?
IMO. Fidele, sir.

    .   .   .   .

BEL. Is not this boy reviv'd from death?
ARV.   One sand another
Not more resembles that sweet rosy lad,
Who died, and was Fidele.—What think you?
GUI. The same dead thing alive.
BEL. Peace, peace! see farther; he eyes us not:
    forbear.
Creatures may be alike: were 't he, I am sure
He would have spoke to us.
GUI.   But we saw him dead.
BEL. Be silent; let's see farther.

Imogen, however, does not remain long un-
recognized. Pisanio, the servant and friend of
Leonatus — the same who had provided her
with the disguise of a page, and given her the
sleeping ipoton—reveals her; and she, kneeling at her father's feet, then asks his blessing.

CYM.   My tears, that fall,
Prove holy water on thee! Imogen,
Thy mother's dead.

IMO.   I am sorry for 't, my lord.

CYM. O, she was naught; and 'long of her it
    was
That we meet here so strangely: but her son
Is gone, we know not how, nor where.

PIS.   My lord,
Now fear is from me, I'll speak troth. Lord Cloten,
Upon my lady's missing, came to me
With his sword drawn; foam'd at the mouth, and
    swore
If I discover'd not which way she was gone,
It was my instant death. By accident,
I had a feigned letter of my master's
Then in my pocket, which directed him
To seek her on the mountains near to Milford.
    .   .   .   .   What became of him,
I farther know not.

GUI.   Let me end the story.
I slew him there.

CYM.   Marry, the gods forefend!
I would not thy good deeds should from my lips
Pluck a hard sentence: prithee, valiant youth,
Deny 't again.

GUI.   I have spoke it, and I did it.

CYM. He was a prince.

GUI. A most uncivil one. The wrongs he did
  me
Were nothing prince-like; for he did provoke me
With language that would make me spurn the sea,
If it could so roar to me. I cut off 's head;
And am right glad he is not standing here
To tell this tale of mine.

CYM.   I am sorry for thee.
By thine own tongue thou art condemn'd, and must
Endure our law : thou art dead.

    .   .   .   .

                            Bind the offender,
And take him from our presence.

BEL.   Stay, sir king.
This is better than the man he slew,
As well descended as thyself; and hath
More of thee merited, than a band of Clotens
Had ever scar for.—Let his arms alone;
                        [*To the* Guard.
They were not born for bondage.

CYM.   Why, old soldier,
Wilt thou undo the worth thou art unpaid for,
By tasting of our wrath? How of descent
As good as we?

ARV.   In that he spoke too far.

CYM. And thou shall die for 't.

Bel.   We will die all three:
But I will prove that two on's are as good
As I have given out him.—My sons, I must
For mine own part unfold a dangerous speech,
Though, haply, well for you.

Arv.   Your danger's ours.

Gui. And our good his.

Bel.   Have at it, then!
By leave;—Thou hadst, great king, a subject, who
Was call'd Belarius.

Cym.   What of him? he is
A banish'd traitor.

Bel.   He it is that hath
Assum'd this age: indeed, a banish'd man;
I know not how a traitor.

Cym.   Take him hence;
The whole world shall not save him.

Bel.   Not too hot:
First pay me for the nursing of thy sons;
And let it be confiscate all, so soon
As I have receiv'd it.

Cym.   Nursing of my sons!

Bel. I am too blunt, and saucy; here's my
     knee:
Ere I arise, I will prefer my sons;
Then, spare not the old father. Mighty sir,
These two young gentlemen, that call me father,

And think they are my sons, are none of mine:
They are the issue of your loins, my liege,
And blood of your begetting.

    CYM.   How! my issue?

    BEL. So sure as you your father's. I, old Mor-
      gan,
Am that Belarius whom you sometime banish'd.

   .   .   .   .

                        These gentle princes
(For such, and so they are) these twenty years
Have I train'd up; those arts they have, as I
Could put into them; my breeding was, sir, as
Your highness knows. Their nurse, Euriphile,
Whom for the theft I wedded, stole these children
Upon my banishment: I mov'd her to 't;
Having receiv'd the punishment before,
For that which I did then: beaten for loyalty,
Excited me to treason. Their dear loss,
The more of you 'twas felt, the more it shap'd
Unto my end of stealing them. But, gracious sir,
Here are your sons again; and I must lose
Two of the sweet'st companions in the world.
The benediction of these covering heavens
Fall on their heads like dew! for they are worthy
To inlay heaven with stars.

    CYM.   Thou weep'st, and speak'st.
The service that you three have done is more

    8

Unlike than this thou tell'st. I lost my children:
If these be they, I know not how to wish
A pair of worthier sons.

    BEL.   Be pleas'd awhile.—
This gentleman, whom I call Polydore,
Most worthy prince, as yours, is true Guiderius:
This gentleman, my Cadwal, Arviragus,
Your younger princely son; he, sir, was lapp'd
In a most curious mantle, wrought by the hand
Of his queen mother, which, for more probation,
I can with ease produce.

    CYM.   Guiderius had
Upon his neck a mole, a sanguine star:
It was a mark of wonder.

    BEL.   This is he,
Who hath upon him still that natural stamp.
It was wise Nature's end in the donation,
To be his evidence now.

    CYM.   O, what, am I
A mother to the birth of three? Ne'er mother
Rejoic'd deliverance more.—Bless'd may you be,
That, after this strange starting from your orbs,
You may reign in them now.—O Imogen!
Thou hast lost by this a kingdom.

    IMO.   No, my lord;
I have got two worlds by 't.—O, my gentle brothers!
Have we thus met? O, never say hereafter

But I am truest speaker: you call'd me brother,
When I was but your sister; I you, brothers,
When you were so indeed.

CYM.   Did you e'er meet?

ARV. Ay, my good lord.

GUI.   And at first meeting lov'd;
Continued so, until we thought he died.

CYM.   O rare instinct!
When shall I hear all through?

.   .   .   .

The forlorn soldier, that so nobly fought,
He would have well become this place, and grac'd
The thankings of a king.

Then Leonatus declares himself. " I am,
sir," he says, "the soldier that did company
these three in poor beseeming; 'twas a fitment
for the purpose I then follow'd." And Cymbeline, finding himself thus so much indebted
to the two men whom he had unjustly banished, answers: " Pardon's the word to all."
Arviragus, always the more gentle of the
brothers, has a more affectionate welcome for
his sister's husband.

ARV.   You holp us, sir,
As you did mean indeed to be our brother;
Joy'd are we that you are.

While happy Imogen casts the "harmless lightning of her eyes" upon her recovered husband,
her father, and her new-found brothers, "hitting
each object with a joy." And the drama con-
cludes with a peace which the Roman sooth-
sayers declare "the fingers of the powers above
do tune."

CYM.   Laud we the gods!
And let our crooked smokes climb to their nostrils
From our bless'd altars. Publish we this peace
To all our subjects. Set we forward. Let
A Roman and a British ensign wave
Friendly together; so through Lud's town march,
And in the temple of great Jupiter
Our peace we'll ratify.

These two youths, brought up in simple-
hearted goodness, and amid the wildest and
grandest natural scenery, seem alike at first
sight, but they are really far from being so.
Guiderius, the eldest, and the heir to the
throne, is much the more hasty and manly of
the two. He is the successful hunter; it is
he that kills the braggart Cloten; he is impa-
tient with his brother for recalling the pretty
legend of the robin red-breasts covering un-

buried bodies with moss and flowers, and
blames him for playing "in wench-like words
with that which is so serious." Still, his piety
and his loyalty to his father are just as con-
spicuous; and though he longs for the battle-
field, he asks his supposed father's permission
and blessing.

Arviragus is more tender and gentle, more
thoughtful in little matters of kindness and
courtesy. He takes off his shoes for fear of
waking Fidele in the cave; it is he that with
fairest flowers promises to "sweeten thy sad
grave," and "sing him to the ground as once
our mother." And when Imogen is revealed
as his sister, and Leonatus as his brother-in-
law, he is the first with brotherly words to
welcome him.

We must notice, also, how admirably Shakespeare suits the natural scenes to the characters
of the boys. They are made hunters, not shepherds, for a hunter's life is in perfect keeping
with the spirit of adventure in the story, and
with the scenes in which they are afterward to
act. This skillful adaptation is still more re-
markable if the forest scenes in "Cymbeline"
are compared with those of Arden in "As You

Like It." The boys in "Cymbeline" climb mountains and pursue game; in Arden's green glades the characters saunter along pleasant foot-paths, and give themselves to contemplation or love-making amid surroundings whose air is that of rustic ease and beauty. Schlegel says that the forest scenes in "Cymbeline" are capable of inspiring a worn-out imagination with poetry; and the scene in the cave where Imogen meets her unknown brothers is an idyll so charming as can scarcely be written again.

CYMBELINE.

SHAKESPEARE found the historical material for this play in Holinshed's "Chronicles"; and he has adhered to them as far as is consistent with the progress of a romantic story. The following extracts include all in Holinshed that bears upon the plot of the drama:

"After the death of Cassibellane, Theomantius, or Lenantius, the youngest son of Lud, was made king of Britain, in the year of the world 3921, and before the coming of Christ 45 years. . . . . Theomantius ruled the land in good quiet, and paid the tribute to the Romans which Cassibellane had granted, and finally departed this life, after he had reigned twenty-two years, and was buried in London.

"Kymbeline, or Cimbeline, the son of Theo-

mantius, was of the Britons made king, after
the decease of his father, in the year of the
world 3944, and before the birth of our Sa-
viour 33. This man (as some write) was
brought up at Rome, and there made knight
by Augustus Cæsar, under whom he served in
the wars, and was in such favor with him that
he was at liberty to pay his tribute or not.

"Touching the continuance of the years of
Kymbeline's reign some writers do vary, but the
best approved affirm that he reigned thirty-
five years, and then died, and was buried at
London, leaving behind him two sons, Guiderius and Arviragus. But here is to be noted
that, although our histories do affirm that this
Kymbeline, as also his father, Theomantius,
lived in quiet with the Romans, and continually to them paid the tributes which the Brit-
ains had covenanted with Julius Cæsar to pay,
yet we find in the Roman writers that, after
Julius Cæsar's death, when Augustus had taken
upon him the rule of the empire, the Britons
refused to pay that tribute.

.   .   .   .   .   .

"But whether this controversy, which ap-
peareth to fall forth betwixt the Britons and

the Romans, was occasioned by Kymbeline or some other prince of the Britons, I have not to avouch ; for that by our writers it is reported that Kymbeline, being brought up in Rome, and knighted in the court of Augustus, ever showed himself a friend to the Romans, and was chiefly loth to break with them, because the youth of the British nation should not be deprived of the benefit to be trained and brought up among the Romans, whereby they might learn both to behave themselves like civil men and to attain to the knowledge of feats of war. . . . .

"That this was true, it is evident enough in Strabo's words, which are in effect as followeth : ' At this present' (saith he), ' certain princes of Britain, procuring by ambassadors, and dutiful demeanors, the amity of the Emperor Augustus, have offered in the capitol unto the gods gifts or presents, and have ordained the whole isle, in a manner, to be appertinent to the Romans. They are burdened with sore customs which they pay for wars, ... commonly ivory vessels, shears, ouches or earrings, and other conceits made of amber and glasses, and such like manner of merchan-

dise.   So that now there is no need of any
army, or garrison of men of war, to keep the
isle ; for there needeth not past one legion of
footmen, or some wing of horsemen, to gather
up and receive the tribute, for the charges are
rated according to the quantity of the tributes,
. . . . and if any violence were used, it were
dangerous, lest they might be provoked to rebellion.'   Thus far Strabo."

Holinshed's " Chronicle " also furnished
Shakespeare with the name of *Imogen.*   In the
old black-letter it is written *Innogen,* and she
was queen to *Brute,* king of Britain.   In the
same work he also found the name of *Cloten,*
who, when the line of Brute was at an end,
was one of the five kings that governed Britain, Cloten, or Cloton, being king of Cornwall.
Leonatus he probably took from Sidney's "Ar-
cadia."   There Leonatus is the legitimate son
of the blind king of Paphlagonia, on whose
story, many say, the episode of Gloster, Edgar, and Edmund is formed in " King Lear."

THE BOY FOOL

IN KING LEAR.

PERSONS MENTIONED IN THE PLAY.

LEAR.—*King of Britain.*

DUKE OF ALBANY.
DUKE OF CORNWALL. } *Sons-in-Law of the King.*

GLOSTER.
KENT. } *English Lords, Friends of Lear.*

THE FOOL.

EDGAR.—*A Pretended Madman.*

KING OF FRANCE.
DUKE OF BURGUNDY. } *Suitors to Cordelia.*

GONERIL.
REGAN. } *Daughters of King Lear.*
CORDELIA.

King Lear.

The Boy Fool.

THE BOY FOOL

THE play of "King Lear" belongs to the heathen period of British history, but to a time far anteceding that of "Cymbeline." Quite intentionally in this play, Shakespeare has depicted Lear's bursts of rage, Cornwall's cruelties, the rude vehemence of Kent, the unnatural hard-heartedness of Lear's two eldest daughters, for they are the legitimate fruits of an age when impulses had an ungovernable strength, and crime a gigantic enormity.

In "Lear" we have no splendid furniture, and elegant costumes, and Roman courtesy of manners; we must imagine its scenes in narrow chambers of rude masonry, on wild, barren moors, and amid stout Gothic coarseness and barbarity—a heathenish time, when chance reigned above, and power and force below, and when the wicked met death without a pang of remorse. Selfishness and self-will dominate, and the play would be too painful and tragic for perusal, if it were not for the "fairest Cordelia," and for the Fool, a boy who is a gracious emanation of all that is gentle and constant and cheerful and true.

Lear, King of Britain, in the year of the world 3105—eight hundred years before Cymbeline—had three daughters: Goneril, wife to the Duke of Albany; Regan, wife to the Duke of Cornwall; and Cordelia, a young maiden, for whose hand the King of France and the Duke of Burgundy were suitors, and who, at the time the play opens, are staying at the court of Lear. Then the King, being eighty years old, suddenly determines, with "unruly waywardness," to take no further part in the government, and to divide his kingdom among his daughters in such proportions as their love for him seemed to deserve.

Attended by his daughters, Albany, Cornwall, and others, he asks:

Which of you, shall we say, doth love us most?
That we our largest bounty may extend,

Where nature doth with merit challenge.—Goneril,
Our eldest born, speak first.

   Gon. Sir, I love you more than word can wield
      the matter,
Dearer than eyesight, space, and liberty ;
Beyond what can be valued, rich or rare ;
No less than life, with grace, health, beauty, honor :
As much as child e'er lov'd, or father found.
A love that makes breath poor, and speech unable ;
Beyond all manner of so much I love you.

Lear, delighted with this assurance of her
love, and believing that her heart went with
it, in a passion of fatherly fondness bestowed
upon her and her husband Albany one third
of his ample kingdom. Then calling his second daughter, he asked, " What says our dearest
Regan, wife of Cornwall?"

   Reg. I am made of that self metal as my sister,
And prize me at her worth. In my true heart,
I find she names my very deed of love ;
Only she comes too short,—that I profess
Myself an enemy to all other joys,
Which the most precious square of sense possesses ;
And find, I am alone felicitate
In your dear highness' love.

LEAR. To thee, and thine, hereditary ever,
Remain this ample third of our fair kingdom;
No less in space, validity, and pleasure,
Than that conferr'd on Goneril.—Now, our joy,
Although our last and least; to whose young love
The vines of France and milk of Burgundy
Strive to be interess'd; what can you say, to draw
A third more opulent than your sisters? Speak.

But Cordelia, who really loved her father
almost as extravagantly as her sisters pretended
to do, could not with crafty, flattering speeches
sue for extravagant rewards. She declares she
"loves her father according to her duty"; he
has "given her breeding, and cared for her,"
and she says she will

Return those duties back as are right fit,
Obey you, love you, and most honor you.
Why have my sisters husbands, if they say
They love you all? Haply, when I shall wed,
That lord whose hand must take my plight shall carry
Half my love with him, half my care, and duty.

This plain and honest speech greatly enraged Lear. Always rash and passionate, the
dotage of old age had, moreover, clouded his
perceptions: he could not discern truth from

flattery, and in a fury of resentment he divided
the third part of his kingdom, which yet remained, between Cordelia's two elder sisters
and their husbands Albany and Cornwall; in-
vesting them, in the presence of the court,
with the power, revenue, and execution of the
government; only retaining for himself the
name of king, one hundred knights for his attendants, and the right to be maintained with
them, by monthly course, in each of his daughters' palaces in turn.

So foolish a division of his kingdom filled
the court with astonishment and sorrow; but
no one but the Earl of Kent had the courage
to oppose the passionate and self-willed monarch. He says with rude honesty:

—be Kent unmannerly,
When Lear is mad. What wouldst thou do, old man?
.   .   .   .

Reserve thy state;
And, in thy best consideration, check
This hideous rashness: answer my life my judg-
        ment,
Thy youngest daughter does not love thee least,
Nor are those empty-hearted, whose low sounds
Reverb no hollowness.

LEAR.   Kent, on thy life, no more.

KENT. My life I never held but as a pawn
To wage against thine enemies.   .   .

LEAR. Out of my sight!

KENT. See better, Lear; and let me still remain
The true blank of thine eye.

LEAR. Now, by Apollo,—

KENT.   Now, by Apollo, king,
Thou swear'st thy gods in vain.

This honest freedom of Kent is, however, useless. Lear, in a frantic anger, allots him five days to prepare for exile, and declares, if on the tenth day following he be found in his dominions, "the moment is thy death." To the King, Kent says, "Fare thee well, king"; to Cordelia, "The gods to their dear shelter take thee, maid"; and so departs.

Then the King of France and the Duke of Burgundy are called in, to hear the determination of Lear to disinherit his youngest daughter. Lear asks them, if now that she is "unfriended, and dower'd with his curse," they will "take her, or leave her"? Burgundy will take no wife on such conditions, but the King of France, on understanding wherein she has offended, the not being able to flatter, answers:

France. Fairest Cordelia, thou art most rich, be-
    ing poor;
Most choice, forsaken; and most lov'd, despis'd!

.   .   .   .   .   .

Thy dowerless daughter, king, thrown to my chance,
Is queen of us, of ours, and our fair France.

The Third Scene of the First Act takes us
to the Duke of Albany's palace. The first
month is not over, yet already his eldest,
Goneril, "with the wolfish visage, and the
dark frontlet of ill-humor," is beginning to
show her true character. She asks her steward:

Did my father strike my gentleman for chiding of
    his fool?
  Stew. Ay, madam.
  Gon. By day and night he wrongs me; every
    hour
He flashes into one gross crime or other,
That sets us all at odds: I'll not endure it,
His knights grow riotous, and himself upbraids us
On every trifle:—When he returns from hunting
I will not speak with him; say, I am sick:—
If you come slack of former services
You shall do well; the fault of it I'll answer.

Put on what weary negligence you please,
You and your fellows; I'd have it come to ques-
    tion:
If he distaste it, let him to my sister,
Whose mind and mine, I know, in that are one,
   .   .   .   .   Idle old man,
That still would manage those authorities
That he hath given away!—Now by my life,
Old fools are babes again; and must be us'd
With checks, as flatteries,—   .   .   .

   .   .   .   .

And let his knights have colder looks among
you; what grows of it no matter; advise your fellows so (I would breed from hence occasions, and
I shall, that I may speak):—I'll write straight to my
sister, to hold my course.

People are generally unwilling to believe
the unpleasant consequences which their own
mistakes and obstinacy bring on them; and
Lear shut his eyes to his daughter's behavior
as long as he could. But the steward, following Goneril's instructions, takes the first opportunity of being insolent to Lear, and the old
king, with characteristic passion, strikes him.
Then Kent, who, though banished on pain of
death, has followed the King in the disguise of

a servant, throws the fellow and orders him away.

But Lear is much disturbed. He repeated-ly calls for his Fool, that he may divert the current of his sad and anxious thoughts. He says to one of his knights: " I have perceived a most faint neglect of late;—I will look fur-ther into it. But where's my Fool? I have not seen him this two days."

KNIGHT. Since my young lady's going into France, sir, the fool hath much pined away.

LEAR. No more of that; I have noted it well.

These two remarks are the key to the whole tender connection between Lear and his boy Fool. They show us how the boy's loving, gentle nature clung to the "sweetest Cordelia"; and we are aware that the King's sympathy with it is the one unselfish and redeeming spot in the old passionate monarch's breast. And after this, through all his melancholy wanderings, his care of the Fool is constant and loving. In his explosions of rage and invec-tive, he never forgets his faithful companion's tenderness. The unkindness of his daughters, the unpitying elements, can not quench this spark of love in his wretched heart. In the depths of his misery, he turns from his own sufferings to think of him:

Poor fool and knave, I have one part in my heart
That's sorry yet for thee.

The word "knave" signifies only a "boy." It is a Saxon word which has gradually come to have a much worse meaning. The constancy of attachment between the two opposite natures of Lear and his Fool is one of the most beautiful and masterly creations that ever entered the mind of any poet. The "poor knave's" struggles between his "*heart's sadness*" and his "*duty's jesting*" form a vivid self-contrast, while his evidently forced humor is a powerful heightening of the mournful and tragic in the play. Thus, we are no sooner made to feel the affectionate tenderness of the lad's character, by hearing, just before his first entrance, that since Cordelia's "going into France the fool hath much pined away," than we see him come in with a playful manner, assumed to hide his concern from his old master; and, from that time to the close, he maintains a constant endeavor by sportive words to veil his profound interest and sorrow in all that takes place.

Enter FOOL.

FOOL. (*To* KENT, giving him his cap.) Let me hire him, too:—here's my coxcomb.

LEAR. How now, my pretty knave! how dost thou?

FOOL. Sirrah, you were best take my coxcomb.

LEAR. Why, my boy?

FOOL. Why? For taking one's part that's out of favor.—Nay, an thou canst not smile as the wind sits, thou'lt catch cold shortly: there, take my coxcomb. Why, this fellow has banish'd two on's daughters, and did the third a blessing against his will: if thou follow him, thou must needs wear my coxcomb.—How now, nuncle! Would I had two coxcombs, and two daughters!

LEAR. Why, my boy?

FOOL. If I gave them all my living, I'd keep my coxcombs myself. There's mine; beg another of thy daughters.

LEAR. Take heed, sirrah; the whip!

FOOL. Truth's a dog must to kennel: he must be whipped out.—

LEAR. A pestilent gall to me.

FOOL. Sirrah, I'll teach thee a speech.

LEAR. Do.

Fool. Mark it, nuncle:—

    Have more than thou showest,
    Speak less than thou knowest,
    Lend less than thou owest,
    Ride more than thou goest,
    Learn more than thou trowest,
    Set less than thou throwest;
    Leave thy drink, ...
    And keep in-a-door,
    And thou shalt have more
    Than two tens to a score.

Lear. This is nothing, fool.

Fool. Then, 'tis like the breath of an unfee'd lawyer; you gave me nothing for't. Can you make no use of nothing, nuncle?

Lear. Why, no, boy; nothing can be made out of nothing.

Fool. Pr'ythee, tell him, so much the rent of his land comes to: he will not believe a fool.

Lear. A bitter fool!

Fool. Dost thou know the difference, my boy, between a bitter fool and a sweet one?

Lear. No, lad; teach me.

Fool. That lord, that counsel'd thee
    To give away thy land,
    Come place him here by me;
    Do thou for him stand:

The sweet and bitter fool
    Will presently appear;
The one in motley here,
    The other found out there.

LEAR. Dost thou call me fool, boy?

FOOL. All thy other titles thou hast given away,
that thou wast born with.

KENT. This is not altogether fool, my lord.

FOOL. No, 'faith; lords and great men will not
let me: if I had a monopoly out, they would
have part on't, and loads too: they will not let
me have all fool to myself; they'll be snatching.
—Give me an egg, nuncle, and I'll give thee two
crowns.

LEAR. What two crowns shall they be?

FOOL. Why, after I have cut the egg i' the middle, and eat up the meat, the two crowns of the
egg. When thou clovest thy crown i' the middle,
and gavest away both parts, thou borest thine ass
on thy back o'er the dirt: thou hadst little wit in
thy bald crown, when thou gavest thy golden one
away. If I speak like myself in this, let him be
whipped that first finds it so.   [*Singing.*

Fools had ne'er less grace in a year;
    For wise men are grown foppish;
And know not how their wits to wear,
    Their manners are so apish.

9

LEAR. When were you wont to be so full of songs, sirrah?

FOOL. I have used it, nuncle, ever since thou madest thy daughters thy mothers; for, when thou gavest them the rod and putt'st down thine own breeches,   [*Singing.*

> *Then they for sudden joy did weep,*
>   *And I for sorrow sung,*
> *That such a king should play bo-peep,*
>   *And go the fools among.*

Pr'ythee, nuncle, keep a schoolmaster that can teach thy fool to lie: I would fain learn to lie.

LEAR. An you lie, sirrah, we'll have you whipped.

FOOL. I marvel, what kin thou and thy daughters are: they'll have me whipped for speaking true, thou'lt have me whipped for lying; and sometimes I am whipped for holding my peace. I had rather be any kind o' a thing than a fool; and yet I would not be thee, nuncle; thou hast pared thy wit o' both sides, and left nothing i' the middle. Here comes one o' the parings.

Enter GONERIL.

LEAR. How now, daughter! What makes that frontlet on?

Methinks, you are too much of late i' the frown.

FOOL. Thou wast a pretty fellow, when thou

hadst no need to care for her frowning; now thou
art an O without a figure. I am better than thou
art now: I am a fool; thou art nothing.—Yes, forsooth, I will hold my tongue! so your face (*to* GONE-
RIL) bids me, though you say nothing.

> Mum, mum,
> He that keeps nor crust nor crum,
> Weary of all, shall want some.—

That's a shealed peascod.   [*Pointing to* LEAR.

GON. Not only, sir, this your all-licensed fool,
But other of your insolent retinue
Do hourly carp and quarrel; breaking forth
In rank and not-to-be-endured riots. Sir,
I had thought, by making this well known unto you,
To have found a safe redress, but now grow fearful,
By what yourself too late have spoke and done,
That you protect this course, and put it on,
By your allowance; which if you should, the fault
Would not 'scape censure, nor the redresses sleep,
Which, in the tender of a wholesome weal,
Might in their working do you that offence,
Which else were shame, that then necessity
Will call discreet proceeding.

FOOL. For you trow, nuncle,

> The hedge-sparrow fed the cuckoo so long,
> That it had its head bit off by its young.

So out went the candle, and we were left darkling.

LEAR. Are you our daughter?

GON. I would, you would make use of your good
    wisdom,
Whereof I know you are fraught, and put away
These dispositions, which of late transform you
From what you rightly are.

FOOL. May not an ass know when the cart draws
the horse?—Whoop, Jug! I love thee.

LEAR. Does any here know me?—Why, this is not
Lear: does Lear walk thus? speak thus? Where
are his eyes? Either his notion weakens, or his
discernings are lethargied.—Sleeping or waking?—
Ha! sure 'tis not so.—Who is it that can tell me
who I am?

FOOL. Lear's shadow.

LEAR. I would learn that; for by the marks of
sovereignty, knowledge, and reason, I should be false
persuaded I had daughters.

FOOL. Which they will make an obedient father.

LEAR. Your name, fair gentlewoman?

GON. This admiration, sir, is much o' the savor
Of other your new pranks. I do beseech you
To understand my purposes aright,
As you are old and reverend, should be wise.
Here do you keep a hundred knights and squires;
Men so disorder'd, so debauch'd and bold,
That this our court, infected with their manners,

Shows like a riotous inn: .   .   .   .

.   .   .   The shame itself doth speak
For instant remedy; be, then, desir'd
By her, that else will take the thing she begs,
A little to disquantity your train;
And the remainder, that shall still depend,
To be such men as may besort your age,
Which know themselves and you.

LEAR.   Darkness and devils!
Saddle my horses; call my train together.—
Degenerate bastard! I'll not trouble thee:
Yet have I left a daughter.

.   .   .   .

.

.   .   .   .

GON.   .   .   .   What, Oswald, ho!
You, sir, more knave than fool, after your master.

[*To the* FOOL.

FOOL. Nuncle Lear, nuncle Lear! tarry, and take
the fool with thee.

A fox, when one has caught her,
And such a daughter,
Should sure to the slaughter,
If my cap would buy a halter;
So the fool follows after.

.   .   .   .

.   .   .   .

SCENE V.—*Enter* LEAR, KENT, *and* FOOL.

LEAR. Go you before to Gloster with these letters.
Acquaint my daughter no farther with anything you
know, than comes from her demand out of the letter. If your diligence be not speedy, I shall be
there before you.

KENT. I will not sleep, my lord, till I have delivered your letter.   [*Exit.*

FOOL. If a man's brains were in 's heels, were 't
not in danger of kibes?

LEAR. Ay, boy.

FOOL. Then, I pr'ythee, be merry; thy wit shall
not go slip-shod.

LEAR. Ha, ha, ha!

FOOL. Shalt see, thy other daughter will use thee
kindly; for though she's as like this, as a crab is
like an apple, yet I can tell what I can tell.

LEAR. What canst tell, boy?

FOOL. She will taste as like this, as a crab does
to a crab. Thou canst tell why one's nose stands
i' the middle on's face?

LEAR. No.

FOOL. Why, to keep one's eyes of either side 's
nose; that what a man can not smell out, he may
spy into.

LEAR. I did her wrong.—

FOOL. Canst tell how an oyster makes his shell?

LEAR. No.

FOOL. Nor I neither; but I can tell why a snail has a house.

LEAR. Why?

FOOL. Why, to put his head in; not to give it away to his daughter, and leave his horns without a case.

LEAR. I will forget my nature.—So kind a father! —Be my horses ready?

FOOL. Thy asses are gone about 'em. The reason why the seven stars are no more than seven, is a pretty reason.

LEAR. Because they are not eight?

FOOL. Yes, indeed. Thou wouldest make a good fool.

LEAR. To take it again perforce! Monster ingratitude!

FOOL. If thou wert my fool, nuncle, I'd have thee beaten for being old before thy time.

LEAR. How's that?

FOOL. Thou shouldest not have been old before thou hadst been wise.

LEAR. O, let me not be mad, not mad, sweet heaven! Keep me in temper: I would not be mad!—

Enter GENTLEMAN.

How now! Are the horses ready?

Gent. Ready, my lord.

Lear. Come, boy.

So Lear departs to the palace of Regan,
his second daughter ; but the letters announc-
ing his approach, which he had sent by Kent,
were nullified by those which Goneril sent.
Kent, for his plain, passionate devotion to his
master, is put in the stocks by Regan and
her husband, the Duke of Cornwall, and the
sight of his messenger in this insulting position is the first thing which greets Lear when
he arrives at Gloster's castle, where Regan is
staying.

Enter Lear, Fool, *and a* Gentleman.

Lear. Ha!   [*To* Kent *in the stocks.*
Mak'st thou this shame thy pastime?

Kent.   No, my lord.

Fool. Ha, ha! look ; he wears cruel garters.
Horses are tied by the head ; dogs and bears by
the neck ; monkeys by the loins, and men by the
legs ; when a man is over-lusty at legs, then he
wears wooden nether-stocks.

Lear. What's he, that hath so much thy place
      mistook,
To set thee here?

KENT. It is both he and she;
Your son and daughter.

LEAR. No.

KENT. Yes.

LEAR. No, I say.

KENT. I say, yea.

LEAR. No, no; they would not.

KENT. Yes, they have.

LEAR. By Jupiter, I swear, no.

KENT. By Juno, I swear, ay.

LEAR. They durst not do't;
They could not, would not do 't: 'tis worse than
    murder,
To do upon respect such violent outrage.
Resolve me with all modest haste which way
Thou might'st deserve, or they impose, this usage,
Coming from us.

KENT. My lord, when at their home
I did commend your highness' letters to them,
Ere I was risen from the place that show'd
My duty kneeling, came there a reeking post,
Stew'd in his haste, half breathless, panting forth
From Goneril, his mistress, salutations;
Deliver'd letters, spite of intermission,
Which presently they read: on whose contents,
They summon'd up their meiny,* straight took horse;

* "Meiny"; that is, their retinue or followers.

Commanded me to follow, and attend
The leisure of their answer; gave me cold looks:
And meeting here the other messenger,
Whose welcome I perceiv'd had poison'd mine,
(Being the very fellow which of late
Display'd so saucily against your highness)
Having more man than wit about me, drew:
He rais'd the house with loud and coward cries.
Your son and daughter found this trespass worth
The shame which here it suffers.

    Fool. Winter's not gone yet, if the wild geese fly
      that way.

        Fathers that wear rags,
          Do make their children blind;
        But fathers that bear bags,
          Shall see their children kind.
        Fortune, that arrant maid,
          Ne'er turns the key to the poor.—
But, for all this, thou shalt have as many dolors for
thy daughters, as thou canst tell in a year.

    Lear. O, how this mother swells up toward my
      heart!
Hysterica passio!—down, thou climbing sorrow!
Thy element's below.—Where is this daughter?

    Kent. With the earl, sir; here, within.

    Lear.   Follow me not:
Stay here.   [*Exit.*

GENT. Made you no more offence than what you speak of?

KENT. None.

How chance the king comes with so small a train?

FOOL. An thou hadst been set i' the stocks for that question, thou hadst well deserv'd it.

KENT. Why, fool?

FOOL. We'll set thee to school to an ant, to teach thee there's no laboring i' the winter. All that follow their noses are led by their eyes, but blind men; and there's not a nose among twenty but can smell him that's stinking. Let go thy hold, when a great wheel runs down a hill, lest it break thy neck with following it; but the great one that goes up the hill, let him draw thee after. When a wise man gives thee better counsel, give me mine again : I would have none but knaves follow it, since a fool gives it.

That sir, which serves and seeks for gain,
      And follows but for form,
Will pack when it begins to rain,
      And leave thee in the storm.
But I will tarry; the fool will stay,
      And let the wise man fly:
The knave turns fool that runs away,
      The fool no knave, perdy.

KENT. Where learn'd you this, fool?

FOOL. Not i' the stocks, fool.

Regan and Cornwall at first refused to see Lear; "they are sick—they are weary—they have travel'd far"; and Lear rightly interprets these excuses as "mere fetches, the images of revolt and flying off." He sends still more importunate messages, but with sore and wretched misgivings:

LEAR. O me! my heart, my rising heart!—but, down. ·

FOOL. Cry to it, nuncle, as the cockney* did to the eels, when she put them i' the paste alive; she rapp'd 'em o' the coxcombs with a stick, and cried, "Down, wantons, down!" 'Twas her brother, that in pure kindness to his horse buttered his hay.

Regan is equal to her sister in wickedness. Shakespeare "takes ingratitude," Victor Hugo has said, "and he gives this monster two heads, Goneril and Regan." The two terrible creatures are, however, distinguishable. Goneril, with her "wolfish visage" and the "dark frontlet" of ill-humor is pitilessly, resolutely cruel. Regan is a smaller, shriller, more eager piece of malice. Goneril is the instigator, Regan is

---

* Cockney here means a cook.

her echo. Goneril knows her sister's weakness, so she goes to her, in order to compel
her to co-operate with her. Lear at first as-
sumes her sympathy; he addresses her as
" beloved Regan," and tells her how her sister
" hath tied sharp-tooth'd unkindness, like a vult-
ure," to his heart.

Regan can not think her sister would " fail
her obligation." She cruelly reminds her father
that " he is old, and should be ruled and led
by some discretion that discerns his state better
than his own"; and she advises him to go back
to Goneril and ask her forgiveness. Then Goneril enters, and Regan, taking her by the hand,
urges :

REG. I pray you, father, being weak, seem so.
If, till the expiration of your month,
You will return and sojourn with my sister,
Dismissing half your train, come then to me :
I am now from home and out of that provision
Which shall be needful for your entertainment.
  LEAR. Return to her? and fifty men dismiss'd?
  .   .   .   .
    .   .   .   . Return with her?
Why, the hot-blooded France, that dowerless took
Our youngest born, I could as well be brought

To knee his throne, and, squire-like, pension beg
To keep base life afoot.

    GON.   At your choice, sir.

    LEAR. I prithee, daughter, do not make me mad:
I will not trouble thee, my child; farewell.

    .   .   .   .

Mend, when thou canst; be better, at thy leisure:
I can be patient; I can stay with Regan,
I, and my hundred knights.   .   .   .

    REG.   .   .   .   .   .   .

    .   .   .   .   If you will come to me,
(For now I spy a danger) I entreat you
To bring but five and twenty: to no more
Will I give place, or notice.

    LEAR. I gave you all—

    REG.   And in good time you gave it.

    LEAR. [*To* GONERIL.] I'll go with thee;
Thy fifty yet doth double five and twenty,
And thou art twice her love.

    GON.   Hear me, my lord;
What need you five and twenty, ten, or five,
To follow in a house, where twice as many
Have a command to tend you?

    REG.   What need one?

    LEAR. O! reason not the need: our basest beggars
Are in the poorest thing superfluous.

    .   .   .   .

You heavens, give me that patience, patience I need!
You see me here, you gods, a poor old man,
As full of grief as age; wretched in both:
If it be you that stir these daughters' hearts
Against their father, fool me not so much
To bear it tamely; touch me with noble anger.
 . . . You think, I'll weep;
No, I'll not weep:—
I have full cause of weeping; but this heart
Shall break into a hundred thousand flaws,
Or ere I'll weep.—O fool! I shall go mad.
    [*Exeunt* LEAR, GLOSTER, KENT, *and* FOOL.

CORN. Let us withdraw, 'twill be a storm.
REG. This house is little: the old man and 's
  people
Can not be well bestow'd.
 GON. 'Tis his own blame; h'ath put himself from
  rest,
And must needs taste his folly.
 REG. For his particular, I'll receive him gladly,
But not one follower.
 GON.   So am I purpos'd.
Where is my lord of Gloster?

Re-enter GLOSTER.

GLO. The king is in high rage.
CORN.   Whither is he going?

GLO. He calls to horse; but will I know not
whither.

CORN. 'Tis best to give him way; he leads himself.

GON. My lord, entreat him by no means to stay.

GLO. Alack! the night comes on, and the bleak
    winds
Do sorely ruffle; for many miles about
There's scarce a bush.

REG.   O, sir! to willful men,
The injuries that they themselves procure
Must be their schoolmasters.   Shut up your doors:
        .   .   .   .

CORN. Shut up your doors, my lord; 'tis a wild
    night :
My Regan counsels well.   Come out o' the storm.

A picture of dreadful solemnity is now
before us; the helpless old man cast out by
his children into darkness, storm, and desola-
tion, wanders without shelter, with bare head,
stripped of his last possession, and transformed
from a king into a beggar.

SCENE.—*The Wild Heath.   A Storm raging.*
Enter LEAR *and* FOOL.

LEAR. Blow, winds, and crack your cheeks! rage!
    blow!

You cataracts and hurricanoes, spout,
Till you have drench'd our steeples, drown'd the cocks !
You sulphurous and thought-executing fires,
Vaunt-couriers to oak-cleaving thunder-bolts,
Singe my white head ! And thou, all-shaking thunder,
Strike flat the thick rotundity o' the world !
Crack nature's molds, all germens spill at once,
That make ingrateful man !

FOOL. O nuncle, court holy-water* in a dry house
is better than this rain-water out o' door. Good
nuncle, in, and ask thy daughters' blessing : here's a
night that pities neither wise men nor fools.

LEAR.   .   .   .   Spit fire ! spout, rain !
Nor rain, wind, thunder, fire, are my daughters :
I tax not you, you elements, with unkindness;
I never gave you kingdom, call'd you children,
You owe me no subscription : then, let fall
Your horrible pleasure; here I stand, your slave,
A poor, infirm, weak, and despised old man.
But yet I call you servile ministers,
That will with two pernicious daughters join
Your high-engender'd battles, 'gainst a head
So old and white as this. O ! O ! 'tis foul !

FOOL. He that has a house to put 's head in has
a good head-piece.

* " *Court holie water ;*—compliments, faire words, flattering
speeches."

Enter KENT.

LEAR. No, I will be the pattern of all patience;
I will say nothing.

KENT. Who's there?

FOOL. Marry, here's grace, and a cod-piece;
that's a wise man and a fool.

KENT. Alas, sir! are you here? .   .   .
.   .   .   .   . Since I was man,
Such sheets of fire, such bursts of horrid thunder,
Such groans of roaring wind and rain, I never
Remember to have heard: .   .   .   .

LEAR.   Let the great gods,
That keep this dreadful pother o'er our heads,
Find out their enemies now.   .   .   .
.   .   .   . I am a man
More sinn'd against than sinning.

KENT.   Alack, bare-headed!
Gracious my lord, hard by here is a hovel;
Some friendship will it lend you 'gainst the tempest:
.   .   .   .

LEAR. My wits begin to turn.—
Come on, my boy. How dost my boy? Art cold?
I am cold myself.—Where is this straw, my fellow?
The art of our necessities is strange,
That can make vile things precious. Come, your
    hovel.

Poor fool and knave, I have one part in my heart
That's sorry yet for thee.

Fool. *He that has and a little tiny wit,—*   [*Sings.*
   With heigh, ho, the wind and the rain,—
  Must make content with his fortunes fit ;
   For the rain it raineth every day.

Lear. True, my good boy.—Come, bring us to
 this hovel.

Thus, in the depth of his misery, and in
the rage of the storm, Lear turns from his
own sufferings to care for his Fool:

"Poor fool and knave, I have one part in my heart
 That's sorry yet for thee."

And the kindness and affection are reciprocal,
for, in the opening scene of the storm, when
Kent asks a gentleman, who is with the frantic
King "contending with the fretful elements,"
he is told:

"None but the fool; who labors to out-jest
 His heart-struck injuries."

  A Part of the Heath, with a Hovel.

   Enter Lear, Kent, *and* Fool.

Kent. Here is the place, my lord; good, my
 lord, enter:

The tyranny of the open night's too rough
For nature to endure.

.   .   .   .

    LEAR. Thou think'st 'tis much, that this conten-
       tious storm
Invades us to the skin: so 'tis to thee;
But where the greater malady is fix'd,
The lesser is scarce felt.   .   .   .

    .   .   .   . In such a night
To shut me out!—Pour on; I will endure:—
In such a night as this! O Regan, Goneril!—
Your old kind father, whose frank heart gave all—
O! that way madness lies; let me shun that;
No more of that.   .   .   .   .

    .   .   . But I'll go in:
In, boy; go first.—[*To the* FOOL.] You houseless
       poverty,—
Nay, get thee in. I'll pray, and then I'll sleep.

In this hovel Lear meets a poor, unfortunate noble, who has been compelled to pretend madness in order to escape death; and
the scene between the real and the pretended
madman, with the sad vivacity of the poor
Fool, and the terrors of the raging elements,
form a picture in which we have the very extremes of physical, mental, and moral disorder.

Lear is sure that, in his wretched companion, "nothing could have subdued nature to such lowness, but his unkind daughters," and asks him : "Couldst thou save nothing ? Didst thou give them all ?" The Fool is sure " this cold night will turn us all to fools and madmen."

Gloster mercifully interposes ere long. He says his duty can not suffer him to obey in all Regan and Goneril's harsh commands. He has ventured forth to seek the King and bring him to where both fire and food are ready. But Lear will not go to the shelter Gloster has provided, unless he is accompanied by his new-found fellow-sufferer, whom, in his insane delusion, he regards as a " philosopher," and a "good Athenian"; and Gloster and Kent are compelled to accept the companionship.

Then Lear insists that this man and the Fool are the high justiciaries of the kingdom, before whom he will have Goneril and Regan tried. This change of delusion, and rapid flow of ideas, are faithful symptoms of the acute mania which has seized the King's mind. At every stage of it he recognizes his own madness ; and when the poor Fool asks—

" Prithee, nuncle, tell me, whether a madman be a gentleman, or a yeoman ? "—

Lear answers eagerly :

" A king, a king! "

FOOL. No : he's a yeoman, that has a gentleman to his son ; for he's a mad yeoman, that sees his son a gentleman before him.

 LEAR. It shall be done ; I will arraign them
  straight.—

Come, sit thou here, most learned justicer ;—

 . . . .

I'll see their trial first.—Bring in the evidence.—
Thou robed man of justice, take thy place ;—
    [*To* EDGAR, *the pretended madman.*
And thou, his yoke-fellow of equity, [*To the* FOOL.
Bench by his side.—You are o' the commission,
        [*To* KENT.

 EDG. Let us deal justly.
  Sleepest or wakest thou, jolly shepherd?
   Thy sheep be in the corn.
  And for one blast of thy minikin mouth
   Thy sheep shall take no harm.
Pur ! the cat is gray.

 LEAR. Arraign her first ; 'tis Goneril. I here take my oath before this honorable assembly, she kicked the poor king her father.

On the Heath, in the Storm.

The Boy Fool.

FOOL. Come hither, mistress. Is your name
  Goneril?

LEAR. She can not deny it.

FOOL. Cry you mercy, I took you for a joint-stool.

LEAR. And here's another, whose warp'd looks
  proclaim

What store her heart is made on.—Stop her there!
Arms, arms, sword, fire! Corruption in the place!
False justicer, why hast thou let her 'scape?

EDG. Bless thy five wits!

KENT. O pity!—Sir, where is the patience now,
That you so oft have boasted to retain?

EDG. [*Aside.*] My tears begin to take his part
  so much,
They'll mar my counterfeiting.

LEAR. The little dogs and all,
Tray, Blanch, and Sweet-heart, see, they bark at me.

.   .   .   .

Then let them anatomize Regan, see what breeds
about her heart. Is there any cause in nature, that
makes these hard hearts?   .   .   .   .

KENT. Now, good my lord, lie here, and rest
  awhile.

LEAR. Make no noise, make no noise: draw the
curtains. So, so, so; we'll go to supper i' the morning: so, so, so.

FOOL. And I'll go to bed at noon.

In these, the poor boy's last words, the poet indisputably intended to designate the faithful creature's breaking heart. We see him no more after this scene. Gloster hastily enters, and says to Kent that he has o'erheard a plot for Lear's death, and urges him to hasten away.

There is a litter ready; lay him in 't,
And drive toward Dover, friend, where thou shalt
    meet
Both welcome and protection. Take up thy master:
If thou shouldst dally half an hour, his life,
With thine and all that offer to defend him,
Stand in assured loss.   .   .   .   .
    KENT.   Oppress'd nature sleeps :—
   .   .   .   Come, help to bear thy master;
Thou must not stay behind.   [*To the* FOOL.
  [KENT, GLOSTER, *and the* FOOL *bear off the* KING.

So the dearly loved Fool strangely disappears; his frail existence ceases without sign or comment, except his own pathetic intimation of life closing before its time—"And I'll go to bed at noon."

"What can be said of this Fool? What can be thought of him? Fool he was not in

the sense of lack of wisdom or of knowledge.
He is as individualized and unique as any
character in Shakespeare. He is Jacques with
a cap and bells, and a gay, affectionate temper. He is a spiritualized and poetical Sancho
Panza; and, like him, adds to the sadness of
the tale by the introduction of ridiculous images; for of Lear it may be said, as Byron
said of Don Quixote:

> 'Of all tales 'tis the saddest—and more sad
> Because it makes us laugh.'

"Shakespeare's fools are in all other cases
mere ornaments and appendages to the tale;
but the Fool in Lear is a buttress of the tale.
It is through him Lear first gets into trouble
with his faithful daughter. Lear loves him,
and he loves Cordelia, and his child-like affection for her, his devoted attachment to the
King, his daring contempt for the bad daughters, his insight into the motives of human action, cynical yet tempered by love, render him
a most charming character.

"In physique he is small and weak. His
suffering from exposure to the inclement night
excites Lear's tender compassion, and it does

10

in effect extinguish his frail life. But his powers of intellect are of the finest order. His
wayward rambling of thought may be partly
natural, partly the result of his professed office,
an office then held in no light esteem." Shad-
well might well say of Shakespeare's fools,
that they had more wit than any of the wits
and critics of the time.

Of the Fool in Lear, Mr. Hudson says, our
estimate of the drama as a whole must depend upon the view we take of the Fool—
and this is how he himself understood Lear's
"poor boy": "The soul of pathos in a comic
masquerade; one in whom fun and frolic are
sublimed and idealized into tragic beauty; . . .
his wits are set a-dancing by grief, his jests
bubble up from a heart struggling with pity
and sorrow."

The story of King Lear, after the death of
the Fool, hurries forward to its tragic con-
clusion. He indeed receives succor from his
faithful child, Cordelia, as soon as she has
tidings of his pitiful condition; and, under her
care and love, he in some measure recovers
his reason. But it is a short and flickering
gleam of hope; the army which Cordelia has

brought with her from France to reinstate her father is defeated, and Lear and Cordelia are prisoners in the power of the cruel Goneril and Regan. The concluding events are painfully sad ; Cordelia is treacherously hanged in prison, and Lear dies broken-hearted, lamenting over her:

> Thou'lt come no more.
> Never, never, never, never, never !—
> Pray you undo this button : Thank you, sir.—
> Do you see this? Look on her,—look,—her lips,—
> Look there, look there !—   [*He dies.*
>   EDG. He faints!—My lord, my lord,—

> .   .   .   .

>   KENT. Vex not his ghost: O, let him pass! he
>   hates him
> That would upon the rack of this tough world
> Stretch him out longer.

TRADITIONAL SOURCE OF THE PLOT OF THE PLAY.

THE story of Lear belongs to the popular literature of Europe. It is a pretty episode in the fabulous chronicles of Britain, and whether invented by the monks, or translated from some foreign source, is not very material. The same story is told of Theodosius, "a wise emperor in the city of Rome." Shakespeare found it in his favorite Holinshed; and Holinshed abridged it from the chronicles of Geoffrey of Monmouth. The story, as told by Holinshed, is as follows:

"Leir, the son of Baldud, was admitted ruler over the Britons in the year of the world 3105. At what time Joas reigned as yet in Juda. This Leir was a prince of noble demeanour, governing his land and subjects in great wealth. He made the town of Cairleir, now Leicester, which standeth upon the river of Dore. It is

writ that he had by his wife three daughters,
without other issue, whose names were Gonorilla, Regan, and Cordilla, which daughters he
greatly loved, but especially the youngest, Cordilla, far above the two elder.

"When this Leir was come to great years,
and began to wear unwieldy through age, he
thought to understand the affections of his
daughters towards him, and prefer her whom
he best loved, to the succession of the kingdom. Therefore, he first asked Gonorilla the
eldest, 'how well she loved him'? the which,
calling her gods to record, protested, that she
loved him more than her own life, which by
right and reason should be most dear unto
her. With which answer, the father being well
pleased, turned to the second, and demanded
of her, 'how well she loved him'? Which answered — confirming her sayings with great
oaths—that she loved him more than tongue
could express, and far above all other creatures in the world.

"Then called he his youngest daughter,
Cordilla, before him, and asked of her, 'what
account she made of him'? Unto whom she
made this answer, as followeth:—Knowing the

great love and fatherly kindness you have always borne towards me (for the which, that I may not answer you otherwise than I think, and as my conscience leadeth me), I protest to you, that I have always loved you, and shall continually while I live, love you as my natural father; and if you would more understand of the love that I bear you, ascertain yourself, that so much as you have, so much you are worth, and so much I love you, and no more.

"The father, being nothing content with this answer, married the two eldest daughters, the one unto the Duke of Cornwall, named Henninus, and the other unto the Duke of Albania, called Maglanus; and betwixt them, after his death, he willed and ordained his land should be divided, and the one half thereof should be immediately assigned unto them in hand; but for the third daughter, Cordilla, he reserved nothing.

"Yet, it fortuned that one of the princes of Gallia — which now is called France — whose name was Aganippus, hearing of the beauty, womanhood, and good condition of the said Cordilla, desired to have her in marriage, and

sent over to her father, requiring that he
might have her to wife; to whom answer was
made, that he might have his daughter, but
for any dowry he could have none, for all was
promised and assured to her other sisters already.

"Aganippus, notwithstanding this answer of
denial to receive anything by way of dower
with Cordilla, took her to wife, only moved
thereto (I say) for respect of her person and
amiable virtues. This Aganippus was one of
the twelve kings that ruled Gallia in those
days, as in the British history it is recorded.
But to proceed: after Leir was fallen into
age, the two dukes that had married his two
eldest daughters, thinking it long ere the government of the land did come to their hands,
arose against him in armour, and reft from
him the governance of the land, upon conditions to be continued for term of life: by the
which he was put to his portion; that is, to
live after a rate assigned to him for the main-
tenance of his estate, which in process of time
was diminished, as well by Maglanus as by
Henninus.

"But the greatest grief that Leir took, was

to see the unkindness of his daughters, who
seemed to think, that all was too much which
their father had, the same being never so little,
in so much that, going from the one to the
other, he was brought to that misery, that
they would allow him only one servant to wait
upon him.   In the end, such was the unkindness, or, as I may say, the unnaturalness, which
he found in his two daughters, notwithstanding their fair and pleasant words uttered in
time past, that, being constrained of necessity,
he fled the land, and sailed into Gallia, there
to seek some comfort of his youngest daughter, Cordilla, whom before he hated.

"The Lady Cordilla, hearing he was arrived
in poor estate, she first sent to him privately
a sum of money to apparel himself withall,
and to retain a certain number of servants,
that might attend upon him in honourable
wise, as appertayned to the estate which he
had borne. And then, so accompayned, she
appointed him to come to the court, which he
did, and was so joyfully, honourably, and lovingly received, both by his son-in-law, Aganippus, and also by his daughter, Cordilla, that
his heart was greatly comforted : for he was

no less honoured than if he had been king of the whole country himself. Also, after that he had informed his son-in-law, Aganippus, and his daughter in what sort he had been used by his other daughters, Aganippus caused a mighty army to be put in readiness, and likewise a great navy of ships to be rigged to pass over into Britain, with Leir, his father-in-law, to see him again restored to his kingdom.

" It was accorded that Cordilla should also go with him to take possession of the land, the which he promised to leave unto her, as his rightful inheritor after his decease, notwithstanding any former grants made unto her sisters, or unto their husbands, in any manner of wise ; hereupon, when this army and navy of ships were ready, Leir and his daughter Cordilla, with her husband, took the sea, and arriving in Britain, fought with their enemies, and discomfited them in battle, in the which Maglanus and Henninus were slain, and then was Leir restored to his kingdom, which he ruled after this by the space of two years, and then died, forty years after he first began to reign. His body was buried at Leicester, in a vault under the channel of the river Dore, beneath the town."

The subsequent fate of Cordelia is also related by Holinshed. She became queen after her father's death; but her nephews "levied war against her, and destroyed a great part of the land, and finally took her prisoner, and laid her fast in ward, wherewith she took such grief, being a woman of a manly courage, and despairing to recover liberty, there she slew herself."

Spenser, in the second book of "The Faery Queen," canto x, has also told the story of Leir and his daughters, in six stanzas, in which he has only put in verse the narrative of the chronicle. The concluding stanza will be a sufficient specimen:

"So to his crown she him restor'd again,
　In which he dy'd, made ripe for death by eld,
　And after will'd it should to her remain;
　Who peaceably the same long time did weld,
　And all men's hearts in due obedience held;
　Till that her sister's children, woxen strong,
　Through proud ambition against her rebell'd,
　And overcome, kept in prison long,
　Till weary of that wretched life, herself she hong."

In ballad literature the story has been very beautifully preserved in " Percy's Reliques." Here is found an allusion to Lear's madness, and also to the extravagant cruelty of his daughters. But whether Shakespeare used the ballad for his plot, or the ballad was written after Shakespeare's play, there is nothing to assist us in ascertaining, for the date of the ballad is unknown ; Percy took it from an ancient copy black-letter, entitled "A Lamentable Song of the Death of King Leir and his Three Daughters ":

"King Leir once ruled in this land
    With princely power and peace ;
And had all things with heart's content,
    That might his joys increase.
Amongst those things that nature gave,
    Three daughters fair had he,
So princely seeming, beautiful,
    As fairer could not be.

"So on a time it pleased the king
    A question thus to move,
Which of his daughters to his grace
    Could show the dearest love :

For to my age you bring content,
    Quoth he, then let me hear,
Which of you three in plighted troth
    The kindest will appear.

"To whom the eldest thus began:
    Dear father, mind, quoth she,
Before your face, to do you good,
    My blood shall render'd be;
And for your sake my bleeding heart
    Shall here be cut in twain,
Ere that I see your reverend age
    The smallest grief sustain.

"And so will I, the second said;
    Dear father, for your sake,
The worst of all extremities
    I'll gently undertake:
And serve your highness night and day,
    With diligence and love;
That sweet content and quietness
    Discomforts may remove.

"In doing so, you glad my soul,
    The aged king replied;
But what say'st thou, my youngest girl?
    How is thy love ally'd?

My love (quoth young Cordelia then)
    Which to your grace I owe,
Shall be the duty of a child,
    And that is all I'll show.

"And wilt thou show no more, quoth he,
    Than doth thy duty bind?
I well perceive thy love is small,
    When as no more I find.
Henceforth I banish thee my court,
    Thou art no child of mine;
Nor any part of this my realm
    By favour shall be thine.

"Thy elder sisters' loves are more
    Than well I can demand,
To whom I equally bestow
    My kingdom and my hand,
My pompal state and all my goods,
    That lovingly I may
With those thy sisters be maintain'd
    Until my dying day.

"Thus flattering speeches won renown,
    By these two sisters here;
The third had causeless banishment,
    Yet was her love more dear:

For poor Cordelia patiently
   Went wandering up and down,
Unhelp'd, unpity'd, gentle maid,
   Through many an English town.

"Until at last in famous France
   She gentler fortunes found;
Though poor and bare, yet she was deem'd
   The fairest on the ground:
Where when the king her virtues heard,
   And this fair lady seen,
With full consent of all his court,
   He made his wife and queen.

"Her father, King Leir, this while
   With his two daughters staid;
Forgetful of their promis'd loves,
   Full soon the same decay'd;
And living in Queen Ragan's court,
   The eldest of the twain,
She took from him his chiefest means,
   And most of all his train.

"For, whereas, twenty men were wont
   To wait with bended knee,
She gave allowance but to ten,
   And after scarce to three;

Nay, one she thought too much for him;
    So took she all away,
In hope that in her court, good king,
    He would no longer stay.

"Am I rewarded thus, quoth he,
    In giving all I have
Unto my children, and to beg
    For what I lately gave?
I'll go unto my Gonorell:
    My second child, I know,
Will be more kind and pitiful,
    And will relieve my woe.

" Full fast he hies then to her court;
    Where, when she heard his moan,
Return'd him answer, that she griev'd
    That all his means were gone:
But no way could relieve his wants;
    Yet, if that he would stay
Within her kitchen, he should have
    What scullions gave away.

"When he had heard, with bitter tears,
    He made his answer then:
In what I did, let me be made
    Example to all men.

I will return again, quoth he,
  Unto my Ragan's court;
She will not use me thus, I hope,
  But in a kinder sort.

"Where, when he came, she gave command
  To drive him thence away:
When he was well within her court
  (She said) he would not stay.
Then back again to Gonorell,
  The woeful king did hie,
That in her kitchen he might have
  What scullion boys set by.

"But there of that he was deny'd,
  Which she had promis'd late;
For once refusing, he should not
  Come after to her gate.
Thus, 'twixt his daughters for relief
  He wander'd up and down;
Being glad to feed on beggar's food,
  That lately wore a crown.

"And calling to remembrance then
  His youngest daughter's words,
That said the duty of a child
  Was all that love affords;

But, doubting to repair to her,
    Whom he had banish'd so,
Grew frantic mad; for in his mind
    He bore the wounds of woe:

"Which made him rend his milk-white locks
    And tresses from his head,
And all with blood bestain his cheeks,
    With age and honour spread.

    .   .   .   .   .   .

"Even thus possest with discontents
    He passed o're to France,
In hopes, from fair Cordelia, there
    To find some gentler chance;
Most virtuous dame! which, when she heard
    Of this, her father's grief,
As duty bound, she quickly sent
    Him comfort and relief:

"And by a train of noble peers,
    In brave and gallant sort,
She gave in charge he should be brought
    To Aganippus' court;
Whose royal king, with noble mind,
    So freely gave consent,
To muster up his knights at arms,
    To fame and courage bent.

"And so to England came with speed,
    To repossesse King Leir,
And drive his daughters from their thrones,
    By his Cordelia dear:
Where she, true-hearted, noble queen,
    Was in the battel slain;
Yet he, good king, in his old days,
    Possest his crown again.

"But, when he heard Cordelia's death,
    Who died indeed for love
Of her dear father, in whose cause
    She did this battle move;
He swooning fell upon her breast,
    From whence he never parted:
But on her bosom left his life,
    That was so truly hearted.

"The lords and nobles when they saw
    The end of these events,
The other sisters unto death
    They doomed by consents;
And being dead, their crowns they left
    Unto the next of kin:
Thus have you seen the fall of pride
    And disobedient sin."

It will be seen that Shakespeare has departed from all these authorities in making Lear die, instead of restoring him to his crown and his kingdom. Shakespeare knew better. He, at least, felt that the living martyrdom which Lear had gone through, made a fair dismissal from the stage of life the only decorous thing for him. " As if," says Charles Lamb, " the childish pleasure of getting his gilt robes and scepter again could tempt him to act over again his misused station—as if, at his years, and with his experience, anything was left but to die."

MAMILLIUS AND PERDITA,

CHILDREN OF LEONTES, KING OF SICILY.

PERSONS OF THE PLAY.

LEONTES.—*King of Sicilia.*
MAMILLIUS.—*His Son.*
CAMILLO.
ANTIGONUS. } *Sicilian Lords.*
POLIXENES.—*King of Bohemia.*
FLORIZEL.—*His Son.*
AN OLD SHEPHERD.—*Reputed Father of Perdita.*
HIS SON.
HERMIONE.—*Queen to Leontes.*
PERDITA.—*Daughter to Leontes and Hermione.*
PAULINE.—*Wife to Antigonus.*
MOPSA.
DORCAS. } *Two Shepherdesses.*

MAMILLIUS AND PERDITA,

"A WINTER'S Tale" furnishes us with two most exquisite pictures of youthful life, that of the boy Mamillius, and the maiden Perdita. The scene of this play is laid in Sicilia, and opens with a charming picture of the friendship existing between Leontes, King of Sicily, and Polixenes, King of Bohemia. Camillo, a Sicilian lord, says:

They were trained together in their childhoods; and there rooted betwixt them then such an affection which can not choose but branch now.

Archidamus, a Bohemian lord, then says, he thinks—

there is not in the world either malice or matter to alter it. You have an unspeakable comfort of your

young prince Mamillius; it is a gentleman of the
greatest promise that ever came into my note.

CAM. I very well agree with you in the hopes of
him: It is a gallant child; one that, indeed, physics
the subject, makes old hearts fresh; they that went
on crutches ere he was born, desire yet their life to
see him a man.

But this friendship between the two kings,
that "nothing in the world was to alter," received a shock as sudden as it was unjust.
Polixenes came to visit Leontes at the Sicilian
court, and, after a long stay, when preparing
to return to his own kingdom, was pressed to
remain by Leontes. He refused Leontes positively; but Hermione, the lovely and virtuous
queen of Leontes, by her open, innocent hearti-
ness, induced him to remain.—"Come," she said,

         .   .   .   come, I'll question you
Of my lord's tricks, and yours, when you were boys;
You were pretty lordlings then.

POLIX.   We were, fair queen,
Two lads that thought there was no more behind
But such a day to-morrow as to-day,
And to be boy eternal.

HER. Was not my lord the verier wag o' the two?

POLIX. We were as twinn'd lambs, that did frisk
    i' the sun,
And bleat the one at the other: What we chang'd
Was innocence for innocence; we knew not
The doctrine of ill-doing, nor dreamed
That any did: Had we pursued that life,
And our weak spirits ne'er been higher rear'd
With stronger blood, we should have answer'd heaven
Boldly, "Not guilty"; the imposition clear'd,
Hereditary ours.

That Polixenes should remain at the request of Hermione, after refusing his own en-
treaties, was actually all the cause Leontes had
for suspecting his queen of preferring his
friend to himself. But this suspicion once
harbored, grew, as all evil thoughts do grow,
with unreasonable rapidity and strength; and
the true friend and loving husband was rapidly transformed by them into a cruel and unjust monster.

His first step was to send for Camillo, and
after reciting to him his supposed wrongs and
his doubts, he bade him "bespice a cup, to give
his enemy a lasting wink"; and Camillo, finding all reasoning with the mad jealousy of
Leontes vain, agrees to poison Polixenes—his

11

office of cup-bearer giving him a ready opportunity.

But this promise was but a *ruse* to gain
time. Camillo had no intention of becoming a
partner in Leontes's insane revenge; he warned
Polixenes of his danger, and fled with him to
Bohemia. The flight was, to the jealous King,
certain confirmation of all his suspicions, and
he determined at once to imprison Hermione.
The Queen was in her own apartment, surrounded by her ladies and the little prince,
Mamillius; and, in the simple scene which follows, Shakespeare "seems to have got at the
very heart of childhood-nature—as he did of
all other nature." One of the ladies says:

> Come, my gracious lord,
> Shall I be your playfellow?
> MAM.   No, I'll none of you.
> 1 LADY. Why, my sweet lord?
> MAM. You'll kiss me hard, and speak to me as if
> I were a baby still.—I love you better.
> 2 LADY. And why so, my lord?
> MAM.   Not for because
> Your brows are blacker; yet, black brows, they
>   say,
> Become some women best, so that there be not

Too much hair there, but in a semicircle,
Or a half-moon made with a pen.

2 LADY. Who taught this?

MAM. I learn'd it out of women's faces.—Pray, now,
What color are your eyebrows?

1 LADY. Blue, my lord.

MAM. Nay, that's a mock: I have seen a lady's
nose
That has been blue, but not her eyebrows.

. . . .

HER. What wisdom stirs amongst you? Come,
sir; now
I am for you again: pray you, sit by us,
And tell's a tale.

MAM. Merry or sad, shall't be?

HER. As merry as you will.

MAM. A sad tale's best for winter.
I have one of sprites and goblins.

HER. Let's have that, good sir.
Come on; sit down:—come on, and do your best
To fright me with your sprites: you're powerful at it.

MAM. There was a man,—

HER. Nay, come, sit down; then on.

MAM. Dwelt by a church-yard.—I will tell it softly;
Yond' crickets shall not hear it.

HER. Come on, then,
And give't me in my ear.

But the child leaves for ever his little tale
unfinished. It is interrupted by the rude and
angry entrance of Leontes, who takes him
from his mother, and sends the innocent Queen
to prison. The precocious and tender boy
can not understand nor endure this grief :

He straight declin'd, droop'd, took it deeply,
Fasten'd and fix'd the shame on't in himself,
Threw off his spirit, his appetite, his sleep,
And downright languish'd.

But neither the sorrow of the young prince,
nor the birth of a princess in the prison, soft-
ens the jealous King's heart. Paulina, the wife
of Antigonus, a Sicilian lord, and one of the
Queen's ladies, ventures to bring the pretty
babe, and lay it at the feet of Leontes. At
first, in his blind rage, he proposes to burn
the unoffending infant ; but afterward he orders Antigonus to carry it

To some remote and desert place quite out
Of our dominions; and . . . leave it
Without more mercy, to its own protection,
And favor of the climate.

The Queen's trial follows this outrage ;
messengers sent to the oracle of Apollo have

returned with a sealed answer regarding the Queen, which is to be read in the open court. This " sealed-up oracle" declares that " Hermione is chaste, Polixenes blameless, Camillo a true subject, Leontes a jealous tyrant, his innocent babe truly begotten; and the King shall live without an heir, if that which is lost be not found."

But jealousy is so outrageous and unreasonable a passion, that not even a voice from the gods can satisfy Leontes. He says:

There is no truth at all i' the oracle.
The sessions shall proceed: this is mere falsehood.

But even as he speaks, a servant enters hastily, crying out:

SERV. My lord the king, the king!
LEON.   What is the business?
SERV. O, sir, I shall be hated to report it:
The prince your son, with mere conceit and fear
Of the queen's speed, is gone.
LEON.   How! gone?
SERV.   Is dead.
LEON. Apollo's angry, and the heavens themselves
Do strike at my injustice. [HERMIONE *faints.*] How
    now there?

PAUL. This news is mortal to the queen:—Look
    down,
And see what death is doing?
  LEON.   Take her hence:
Her heart is but o'ercharged; she will recover.—
I have too much believ'd mine own suspicion:
'Beseech you tenderly apply to her
Some remedies for life.—Apollo, pardon
My great profaneness 'gainst thy oracle!—
I'll reconcile me to Polixenes,
New woo my queen, recall the good Camillo,
Whom I proclaim a man of truth. . . .

But the grief and repentance of Leontes
are too late. Paulina shortly informs him that
Hermione is dead; Mamillius also is dead,
Camillo is an exile, the friendship of Polixenes
lost, and the little daughter, whom now he
would thankfully and lovingly embrace, sent
away by Antigonus—as Paulina passionately
tells him—"to be cast forth to crows."

The ship in which Antigonus carried away
the infant princess was driven upon the coast
of Bohemia; and here Antigonus prepares to
abandon the child:

  ANT.   Come, poor babe:—
I have heard (but not believ'd), the spirits o' the dead

May walk again: if such thing be, thy mother
Appear'd to me last night, for ne'er was dream
So like a waking. To me comes a creature,
    .   .   .   .   in pure white robes,
Like very sanctity, she did approach
My cabin where I lay, thrice bow'd before me,
And, gasping to begin some speech . . . .
Did this break from her: "Good Antigonus,
Since fate, against thy better disposition,
Hath made thy person for.the thrower-out
Of my poor babe, according to thine oath,
Places remote enough are in Bohemia,
There weep, and leave it crying; and, for the babe
Is counted lost for ever, Perdita,
I prithee, call 't."   .   .   .   .
    .   .   .   .   .   .
                     Blossom, speed thee well!
                     [*Laying down the babe.*
There lie; and there thy character:* there these;
                     [*Laying down a bundle.*
Which may, if fortune please, both breed thee pretty,
And still rest thine.

Antigonus never returns to Sicily; he is
slain by a bear after leaving Perdita, and the

* "This description, with the name 'Perdita,' as prescribed
in the dream of Antigonus."

child is speedily found by an old shepherd
and his son.

SHEP. Here's a sight for thee: look thee, a
bearing-cloth for a squire's child! Look thee here:
take up, take up, boy: open 't. So, let's see. It
was told me, I should be rich by the fairies: this
is some changeling.—Open 't: what's within, boy?

SON. You're a made old man: if the sins of
your youth are forgiven you, you're well to live.
Gold! all gold!

SHEP. This is fairy gold, boy, and 'twill prove
so: up with it, keep it close; home, home, the next
way. We are lucky, boy; and to be so still requires
nothing but secrecy.—Let my sheep go:—Come, good
boy, the next way home.

These events close the third act of the play;
and a period of sixteen years is supposed to
have intervened when the next scene begins.
It opens at the court of Polixenes in Bohemia,
where Camillo and Polixenes are conversing of
Leontes (now reconciled to Polixenes) and of
the "loss of his most precious queen and children." Then Polixenes speaks of his own son,
the princely Florizel, and of his late frequent
absences from court, and his duties and exer-

cises ; adding, that he has intelligence that
Florizel " is seldom from the house of a most
homely shepherd ; a man, they say, that from
very nothing, and beyond the imagination of
his neighbors, is grown into an unspeakable
estate."

CAM. I have heard, sir, of such a man, who hath
a daughter of most rare note : . . .

POL. That's likewise part of my intelligence,
but I fear the angle that plucks our son thither.
Thou shalt accompany us to the place, where we
will, not appearing what we are, have some question with the shepherd ; from whose simplicity I
think it not uneasy to get the cause of my son's
resort thither. Prithee, be my present partner in
this business. . . .

CAM. I willingly obey your command.

POL. My best Camillo !—We must disguise our-
selves.

In pursuance of this scheme, Polixenes and
Camillo go to a sheep-shearing festival at the
old shepherd's, over which Perdita presides.
There is nothing, in any poet, more fresh and
youthful, more pastoral and princely, than this
exquisitely grouped scene. " It is like a Gre-
cian bass-relief ; and Perdita's speeches to her

guests are finer than anything of the kind
either in the old or the new world of poetry."
The deserted babe has grown up an innocent
maiden—

> Pure as the fann'd snow, ·
> That's bolted by the northern blast twice o'er—

The unsophisticated child of nature, she can
not endure false colors in men, nor even in
flowers. She loves not "piedness" in flowers.
All she does "smacks of something greater";
when she has put herself in gay attire as
Flora, the royal blood within her stirs, and she
feels "her robe does change her disposition,"
and that she speaks more loftily.

Enter SHEPHERD, *with* POLIXENES *and* CAMILLO *disguised;* CLOWN, MOPSA, DORCAS, *and others.*

Prince Florizel, also disguised in a rustic
habit, is with Perdita, and he says:

FLO.   See, your guests approach:
Address yourself to entertain them sprightly,
And let's be red with mirth.
    SHEP. Fie, daughter! when my old wife liv'd, upon
This day she was both pantler, butler, cook;
Both dame and servant: welcom'd all, serv'd all;

Mamillius and Perdita.

Perdita and Polixenes,

Would sing her song, and dance her turn; now here,
At upper end o' table, now, i' the middle .   .   .

.   .   .   .

Come, quench your blushes; and present yourself
That which you are, mistress o' the feast: come
    on,
And bid us welcome to your sheep-shearing,
As your good flock shall prosper.

   PER.   [*To* POLIX.] Sir, welcome!
It is my father's will I should take on me
The hostess-ship o' the day.—[*To* CAM.] You're
    welcome, sir!
Give me those flowers there, Dorcas.—Reverend sirs,
For you there's rosemary, and rue; these keep
Seeming, and savor, all the winter long:
Grace, and remembrance, be to you both,
And welcome to our shearing!

   POL.   Shepherdess
(A fair one are you), well you fit our ages
With flowers of winter.

.   .   .   .

   PER.   Here's flowers for you;
Hot lavender, mints, savory, marjoram;
The marigold that goes to bed wi' the sun,
And with him rises weeping: these are flowers
Of middle summer, and, I think, they are given
To men of middle age. You are very welcome.

CAM.   I should leave grazing, were I of your flock,
And only live by gazing.

PER.   Out, alas !
You'd be so lean, that blasts of January
Would blow you through and through.—Now, my
          fairest friend,   [*To* FLORIZEL.
I would, I had some flowers o' the spring, that might
Become your time of day ! .   .   . O Proserpina !
For the flowers now, that, frighted, thou lett'st fall
From Dis's wagon ! daffodils,
That come before the swallow dares, and take
The winds of March with beauty ; violets, dim,
But sweeter than the lids of Juno's eyes,
Or Cytherea's breath ; pale primroses,
That die unmarried ere they can behold
Bright Phœbus in his strength ; .   .   .
    .   .   .   .   .   bold oxlips, and
The crown-imperial ; lilies of all kinds,
The flower-de-luce being one. Oh ! these I lack,
To make you garlands of, and, my sweet friend,
To strew him o'er and o'er.   .   .   .
    .   .   .   .   Come, take your flowers,
Methinks, I play as I have seen them do
In Whitsun' pastorals.   .   .   .   .

FLO.   What you do
Still betters what is done. When you speak, sweet,
I'd have you do it ever : when you sing,

I'd have you buy and sell so; so give alms;
Pray so; and, for the ordering your affairs,
To sing them too. When you do dance, I wish you
A wave o' the sea, that you might ever do
Nothing but that; move still, still so,
And own no other function. . . .

. . . .

. . . But come; our dance, I pray.
Your hand, my Perdita. . . . .

POL. This is the prettiest low-born lass that ever
Ran on the green-sward: nothing she does, or seems,
But smacks of something greater than herself;
Too noble for this place.

CAM. He tells her something,
That makes her blood look out. Good sooth, she is
The queen of curds and cream. . . .

A Dance of SHEPHERDS *and* SHEPHERDESSES.

POL. Pray, good shepherd, what fair swain is this
Which dances with your daughter?

SHEP. They call him Doricles, and boasts himself
To have a worthy feeding; but I have it
Upon his own report, and I believe it:
He looks like sooth. He says he loves my daugh-
        ter;
I think so too; for never gaz'd the moon
Upon the water, as he'll stand, and read,

As 't were my daughter's eyes; and, to be plain,
I think there is not half a kiss to choose
Who loves another best.

POL.　　　　　　　　She dances featly.

SHEP. So she does anything, though I report it,
That should be silent.

This delicious scene is interrupted by Polixenes discovering himself. His anger is extreme; he fiercely threatens the shepherd and Perdita, and tells Florizel, if ever again he visits in their cottage, he will bar him from succession to the throne, and count him no longer of his kin. Then, with a peremptory order to Florizel to return to court with Camillo, he leaves the feast.

Perdita preserves throughout the stormy scene a noble self-respect, and forbearing silence; she says she was—

not much afeard; for once, or twice,
I was about to speak, and tell him plainly,
The self-same sun that shines upon his court,
Hides not his visage from our cottage, but
Looks on alike. .　　　.　　　.　　　.　　　.
.　　　.　　　. I'll queen it no inch farther,
But milk my ewes, and weep.

But Florizel will not resign Perdita, and the good Camillo, fearful of consequences, sends Perdita, Florizel, and the shepherd to Sicily, with messages of friendship to Leontes. But they were so closely followed by Polixenes, that even in their first interview—and while Leontes was strangely moved by the resemblance of Perdita to his lost queen, Hermione—Polixenes and Camillo arrive at the court of Leontes. However, the old shepherd had heard enough to arouse his suspicions; when he knew Leontes had lost a daughter, who was exposed in infancy, he fell to comparing the time, and to showing the mantle and jewels, and other tokens, which proved that Perdita was indeed the daughter of Leontes, and heiress of the Sicilian crown.

Before the Palace.

1 GENT. I was by at the opening of the fardel; heard the old shepherd deliver the manner how he found it: whereupon, after a little amazedness, we were all commanded out of the chamber; only this, methought I heard the shepherd say, he. found the child.

A PEDDLER PEASANT. I would most gladly know the issue of it.

1 GENT. I make a broken delivery of the business; but the changes I perceived in the king and Camillo were very notes of admiration: they seemed almost, with staring on one another, to tear the cases of their eyes; there was speech in their dumbness, language in their very gesture; they looked, as they had heard of a world ransomed, or one destroyed.

.   .   .   .

Enter another GENTLEMAN.

Here comes a gentleman, that, happily, knows more. —The news, Rogero?

2 GENT. Nothing but bonfires. The oracle is fulfilled; the king's daughter is found: such a deal of wonder is broken out within this hour, that balladmakers can not be able to express it.

Enter a Third GENTLEMAN.

Here comes the lady Paulina's steward; he can deliver you more. . . . . Has the king found his heir?

3 GENT. Most true, if ever truth were pregnant by circumstance: . . . . The mantle of Queen Hermione:—her jewel about the neck of it:—the letters of Antigonus, found with it, which they knew to be his character; the majesty of the creature, in resemblance of the mother;—the affection of nobleness, which nature shows above her breeding, and

many other evidences, proclaim her, with all cer
tainty, to be the king's daughter.

The last surprise of the drama is reserved
for the final act.   Paulina discovers to the repentant King Leontes that Hermione is not
dead.   Out of pious resignation to the oracle,
she had kept apart from her husband until the
lost child was found again; but now they are
blissfully reunited, and Perdita, kneeling to her
long-lost mother, hears her say:

HER.   You gods, look down,
And from your sacred vials pour your graces
Upon my daughter's head!—Tell me, mine own,
Where hast thou been preserv'd? where liv'd? how
          found
Thy father's court? for thou shalt hear, that I,
Knowing by Paulina that the oracle
Gave hope thou wast in being, have preserv'd
Myself, to see the issue.

ORIGIN OF "A WINTER'S TALE."

SHAKESPEARE took the plot of this drama from a tale published by Robert Greene, in A. D. 1588, called "Pandosto; The Triumph of Time," better known as the "History of Dorastus and Fawnia"; a work of extraordinary popularity, fourteen editions being known to exist. The action of the tale and the play is almost identical; only, Shakespeare preserves his injured queen, to be reunited to her daughter after years of solitude and suffering. Greene also makes the queen's young son die of grief during her trial, but Greene only mentions his existence and death. The dramatic exhibition of Mamillius, and the tenderness of the child, belong entirely to Shakespeare. It is one of the most charming and pitiful of Shakespeare's child-pictures, and it requires all the subsequent charm of Perdita to put the poor boy out of our thoughts.

SHAKESPEARE'S WORKS.

Mary Cowden Clarke's Edition.

With a scrupulous revision of the Text. 50 Illustrations. Royal 8vo. Half calf, extra, $12.00; mor. antique, $15.00.

Two Volumes 8vo Edition.

Half calf, extra, $18.00; morocco antique, $25.00.

Four Volumes 8vo Edition.

Cloth, $12.00; half morocco, or half calf, extra, $20.00; full morocco antique, $25.00.

One Volume 8vo Edition.

Half calf, $8.00; morocco antique, $10.00.

Cheap Edition.

With Steel Plates. 8vo. Sheep, $3.50.

Charles Knight's Stratford Shakespeare.

With Life by the Editor. New edition. Large paper. 6 vols., 8vo. Cloth, $10.00; half morocco, or half calf, extra, $20.00; full calf, $24.00; tree calf, extra, $25.00.

A Midsummer-Night's Dream.

Illustrated with 80 Engravings on Wood, printed in black and tints, from drawings by Alfred Fredericks. 4to. Cloth, $5.00; morocco, $10.00.

D. APPLETON & CO., Publishers, 1, 3, & 5 Bond Street, N. Y.

THE GLOBE EDITION OF THE POETS.

Printed on Tinted Paper, and bound in a uniform Green Cloth Binding.

Price, $1.25 per volume.

Any Volume sold separately.

Volumes already published:

CAMPBELL,	DANTE,	KIRKE WHITE,
SCOTT,	TASSO,	SPENSER,
POPE,	BURNS,	BUTLER,
DRYDEN,	COWPER,	HERBERT,
MILTON,	CHAUCER,	MRS. HEMANS,

(2 vols.)

THE POPULAR EDITION OF THE

STANDARD POETS.

SIXTY CENTS A VOLUME.

Volumes already published:

I. Scott's Poetical Works.

II. Milton's Poetical Works.

III. Burns's Poetical Works.

IV. Dante's Poems.

V. Tasso's Jerusalem Delivered.

VI. Campbell's Poetical Works.

VII. Pope's Poetical Works.

VIII. Dryden's Poetical Works.

IX. Kirke White's Poetical Works.

Either of the above sent free by mail, to any address, on receipt of price.

New York: D. APPLETON & CO., 1, 3, & 5 Bond Street.

THE
HOUSEHOLD BOOK OF POETRY.

Collected and Edited by CHARLES A. DANA.

Illustrated with Steel Engravings by Celebrated Artists.

Royal 8vo. Cloth, gilt extra, $5.00; half calf, $8.00; morocco, antique,
$10.00; crushed levant $15.00.

CHEAP EDITION.
Cloth, extra, red edges, $3.50; French morocco, $7.00.

"The purpose of this book is to comprise within the bounds of a single volume whatever is truly beautiful and admirable among the minor poems of the English language. . . . Especial care has also been taken to give every poem entire and unmutilated, as well as in the most authentic form which could be procured."—*Extract from Preface.*

"This work is an immense improvement on all its predecessors. The editor, who is one of the most erudite of scholars, and a man of excellent taste, has arranged his selections under ten heads, namely : Poems of Nature, of Childhood, of Friendship, of Love, of Ambition, of Comedy, of Tragedy and Sorrow, of the Imagination, of Sentiment and Reflection, and of Religion. The entire number of poems given is about two thousand, taken from the writings of English and American poets, and including some of the finest versions of poems from ancient and modern languages. The selections appear to be admirably made, nor do we think that it would be possible for any one to improve upon this collection."—*Boston Traveller.*

"Within a similar compass, there is no collection of poetry in the language that equals this in variety, in richness of thought and expression, and of poetic imagery."—*Worcester Palladium.*

"This is a choice collection of the finest poems in the English language, and supplies in some measure the place of an extensive library. Mr. Dana has done a capital service in bringing within the reach of all the richest thoughts that grace our standard poetical literature."—*Chicago Press.*

"A work that has long been required, and, we are convinced from the selections made, and the admirable manner in which they are arranged, will commend itself at once to the public."—*Detroit Advertiser.*

"Never was a book more appropriately named. By the exercise of a sound and skillful judgment, and a thorough familiarity with the poetical productions of all nations, the compiler of this work has succeeded in combining, within the space of a single volume, nearly every poem of established worth and compatible length in the English language."—*Philadelphia Journal.*

"It is almost needless to say that it is a mine of poetic wealth."—*Boston Post.*

D. APPLETON & CO., Publishers, 1, 3, & 5 Bond Street, N. Y.

WILLIAM CULLEN BRYANT'S WORKS.

Illustrated 8vo Edition of Bryant's Poetical Works.

100 Engravings by Birket Foster, Harry Fenn, Alfred Fredericks, and other Artists. 8vo. Cloth, gilt side and edge, $4.00; half calf, marble edge, $6.00; full morocco, antique, $8.00; tree calf, $10.00.

Household Edition.

12mo. Cloth, $2.00; half calf, $4.00; morocco, $5.00; tree calf, $5.00.

Red-Line Edition.

With 24 Illustrations, and Portrait of Bryant, on Steel. Printed on tinted paper, with red line. Square 12mo. Cloth, extra, $2.50; half calf, $4.00.

Blue-and-Gold Edition.

18mo. Cloth, gilt edge, $1.50: tree calf, marble edge, $3.00; morocco, gilt edge, $4.00.

Letters from Spain and other Countries.

12mo. $1.25.

The Song of the Sower.

Illustrated with 42 Engravings on Wood, from Original Designs by Hennessy, Fenn, Winslow Homer, Hows, Griswold, Nehlig, and Perkins. New cheap edition. Cloth, extra gilt, $2.00.

The Story of the Fountain.

With 42 Illustrations by Harry Fenn, Alfred Fredericks, John A. Hows, Winslow Homer, and others. New cheap edition. Cloth, extra gilt, $2.00.

The Little People of the Snow.

Illustrated with exquisite Engravings, printed in Tints, from Designs by Alfred Fredericks. Cloth, $2.00; morocco, $5.00.

For sale by all booksellers; or sent by mail, post-paid, on receipt of price.

New York: D. APPLETON & CO., 1, 3, & 5 Bond Street.

THE RHYMESTER;

Or, THE RULES OF RHYME.

A Guide to English Versification. With a Dictionary of Rhymes, an Examination of Classical Measures, and Comments upon Burlesque, Comic Verse, and Song-Writing.

By the late TOM HOOD.

Edited, with Additions, by ARTHUR PENN.

18mo, cloth, extra. Uniform with "The Orthoepist" and "The Verbalist." Price, $1.00.

Three whole chapters have been added to the work by the American editor —one on the sonnet, one on the *rondeau* and the *ballade*, and a third on other fixed forms of verse; while he has dealt freely with the English author's text, making occasional alterations, frequent insertions, and revising the dictionary of rhymes.

"Its chapters relate to matters of which the vast majority of those who write verses are utterly ignorant, and yet which no poet, however brilliant, should neglect to learn. Though rules can never teach the art of poetry, they may serve to greatly mitigate the evils of ordinary versification. This instructive treatise contains a dictionary of rhymes, an examination of classical measures, and comments on various forms of verse-writing. We earnestly commend this little book to all those who have thoughts which can not be expressed except in poetic measures."—*New York Observer.*

"If young writers will only get the book and profit by its instructions, editors throughout the English-speaking world will unite in thanking this author for his considerate labor."—*New York Home Journal.*

"This little book was written by the only son of the famous Thomas Hood. He was one of the editors of London 'Fun.' He inherited much of his father's literary vein, now delicate, tender, and fanciful, now satiric, and anon bringing tears with its unutterable pathos. Mr. Hood died in 1874.

"The scope of the little book before us is well defined in its title-page, quoted above. The author believes that systematic rhyme-making is a strong educational power, that it will teach young people to pronounce correctly, etc. The small, quaint volume will be valuable to verse-makers. The chapters treat of verse generally, of classic versification, of feet and cæsura, meter, rhythm and rhyme, of burlesque and comic verse, *vers de société*, of song-writing, of the sonnet, rondeau, ballad, and other fixed forms of verse. Finally, most welcome to budding poetical genius, there is a copious dictionary of rhymes."—*Cincinnati Commercial.*

"Every woman of culture in the United States should not only own, but take to her heart this guide to versification, for every woman of culture is supposed to have the knack of rhyming, and yet, with some few exceptions, a woman's poem can be told from a man's by its disregard of the laws of rhythm. It is a most excellent little manual, and will save many prayers to the Muses."—*Philadelphia Press.*

"In the same series that gave us 'The Orthoëpist' and 'The Verbalist,' we have now 'The Rhymester; or, The Rules of Rhyme, a Guide to English Versification.' The English author was a son of the Thomas Hood, of the 'Song of the Shirt,' dying in 1874. He was a true versifier, and this work was devised as a help to his brethren. It is full of useful suggestion, and can not fail in helpfulness to all who attempt verse. The American editor has happily adapted it to our local needs."—*Boston Commonwealth.*

For sale by all booksellers; or sent by mail, post-paid, on receipt of price.

New York: D. APPLETON & CO., 1, 3, & 5 Bond Street.

Poets and Poetical Works.

Shakespeare from an American Point of View;

Including an Inquiry as to his Religious Faith and to his Knowledge of Law; with the Baconian Theory considered. By GEORGE WILKES. Third edition, revised and corrected by the author. 8vo, cloth, $3.50.

Homes and Haunts of our Elder Poets.

Consisting of Biographical and Descriptive Sketches of Bryant, Emerson, Longfellow, Whittier, Holmes, and Lowell. By R. H. STODDARD, F. B. SANBORN, and H. N. POWERS. With Portraits and numerous Illustrations engraved on wood in the best manner. Exquisitely printed on toned paper. Imperial 8vo, cloth, extra gilt, $5.00.

Fitz-Greene Halleck's Poetical Works.

Edited by JAMES GRANT WILSON.

Complete Poetical Works. 12mo, cloth, $2.50; half calf, extra, $4.50; morocco, antique, $6.00.
Large-paper Copy of the same. 8vo, cloth, $10.00; morocco, antique, $15.00.
Complete Poetical Works. 18mo, in blue-and-gold, $1.00; morocco, antique, $3.00.

English Classics:

A series of small volumes, elegantly printed, consisting of works in English literature acknowledged as classics. Now ready:

English Odes. Collected by E. W. GOSSE.
In Memoriam. By ALFRED TENNYSON.
The Princess. By ALFRED TENNYSON.
Shakespeare's Sonnets. Edited by EDWARD DOWDEN.

With Frontispiece on India paper. 18mo, cloth, green-and-gold, $1.00 each.

The Song Wave:

A Collection of Choice Music, with Elementary Instruction. For the School-Room, Institute-Hall, and Home Circle. 8vo, boards, 80 cts.

Containing a brief, practical, and comprehensive course of elementary instruction, with a great variety of selections, adapted to all occasions, including standard favorites and many new songs.

Die Anna-lise:

A German Play by Hermann Hersch, with an Interlinear Translation, and Directions for learning to read German. By C. F. KROEH, A. M., Professor of Modern Languages in the Stevens Institute of Technology. 12mo, cloth, $1.00.

For sale by all booksellers; or sent by mail, post-paid, on receipt of price.

D. APPLETON & CO., Publishers, 1, 3, & 5 *Bond Street, N. Y.*

www.ingramcontent.com/pod-product-compliance
Lightning Source LLC
Chambersburg PA
CBHW021056030726
47496CB00006B/1864